HOT SEX COOL EROTICA
Stories of Pleasure and Fantasy

ALSO BY BEBE WILDE

Girlfriend of a Surfer: A Novel

Sleeping Around: A Novel

Adults Only: Seven Erotica Shorts

Adults Only: Seven Erotica Shorts - Volume 2

Adults Only: Seven Erotica Shorts - Volume 3

Sex Story: An Erotica Short

Sex Story - Part 2: An Erotica Short

Sex Story - Part 3: An Erotica Short

Love Hurts: A BDSM Erotica Short

A Hot Fireman: An Erotica Short

A Little Bit Submissive

A Little Bit Rough

A Little Bit Controlling

The A Little Bit Trilogy Bundle

You, Me and Him: A Ménage Erotica Short

Cold Hard Cash: A Story of Erotica

Sexual Tension: A BDSM Erotica Story

The Weaker Sex: BDSM Erotica

Merci: A Story of Erotica, Sex and Romance

At the End of the Day: An Office Sex Erotica Short

On the Same Page: An Office Sex Erotica Story

BEBE WILDE

HOT SEX COOL EROTICA
Stories of Pleasure and Fantasy

ABERNATHY and MONROE

Dedication: For those who like more of a good thing.

This edition published in 2014 by Abernathy and Monroe.

At the End of the Day: An Office Sex Erotica Short. Copyright © 2012 by Bebe Wilde.

On the Same Page: An Office Sex Erotica Story. Copyright © 2012 by Bebe Wilde.

Cold Hard Cash: A Story of Erotica. Copyright © 2012 by Bebe Wilde.

Love Hurts: A BDSM Erotica Short. Copyright © 2013 by Bebe Wilde.

You, Me and Him: A Ménage Erotica Short. Copyright © 2012 by Bebe Wilde.

Merci: A Story of Erotica, Sex and Romance. Copyright © 2012 by Bebe Wilde.

Paperback ISBN-13: 978-1-938107-62-7
Paperback ISBN-10: 1-938107-62-4

Published by Abernathy and Monroe.

eBook ISBN–13: 978-1-938107-59-7
eBook ISBN–10: 1-938107-59-4

CONTENTS

At the End of the Day

It had nothing to do with my boyfriend. No, no, and no. It wasn't about him or us or our plans for the future. Life was good. We had a nice little mid-town apartment. We talked about marriage but weren't engaged. We talked about having kids and getting a dog. However, none of this had come to fruition. Our life together included dinners with friends, running together in the park and mulling over bills at the end of the month. It wasn't an exciting life we were leading, but it was nice. It was comfortable. It was nothing like my life at work. At the end of the day, at least.

Was it wrong? Probably. Could I help myself? Absolutely not.

He was British and worked on the floor above me. No, I'm not talking about my boyfriend. We met in the elevator. He told me his company had transferred him from London. It was very fascinating. *Who was this guy?* He was very good looking in a dark eyed, dark haired businessman kind of way. He told me I was beautiful and I blushed. I looked good, I knew that, and I was glad someone appreciated the effort I put into my outfits, the pencil skirts, the black leather stilettos and the crisp white button-down shirts. I wore my hair up in a chignon and what my boyfriend would call nerd glasses—big, black frames that made me look smart. And I was smart. I was over the sales department and people who get those kinds of jobs usually aren't dummies.

It started that day, in the elevator. Just a little flirting, no more, no less. I loved the way he talked; he was smoking hot and the accent made him even more so. He laughed a nice, deep laugh and his eyes sparkled whenever he thought he'd said something funny. I could have listened to him all day long. During the day, I would fantasize about us, about what we would do after everyone else had gone home. I would fantasize about him fucking me across my desk, or across his. I would get hot just thinking about what he was going to do to me and I to him. Hot, hot, hot. So hot, I felt like masturbating, touching myself, even if I was in a meeting with a bunch of suits. It was hard to keep my mind on my work when I knew he was one floor above me, walking around, perhaps telling jokes and thinking about what he and I would be up to later.

I didn't plan on sleeping with him at all. We had just met on the elevator and he told me he loved my shoes, my entire outfit, that it reminded him of the ladies from the sixties that were so hot. He talked about how much care they put into the way they dressed and their hair and he thought I looked like I'd just stepped off a page of a magazine. I laughed and told him I was way too short for that. Five-foot-three doesn't make a model. He told me I looked taller but when he stood next to me he could see that I was this smaller woman, this petite little thing. He liked that. He liked that a lot. He said it was like I was doing a magic trick on him. It made him feel bigger than he was. He was about six-foot himself.

When the elevator stopped on my floor first, he grabbed me by the elbow and told me it was nice to meet me.

"But I haven't told you my name," I said.

"Then what is it?"

"Chloe," I said and smiled.

"I'm Ted, Chloe," he said. "Nice to meet you."

And *you*, I thought. It *was* nice of us to meet. I nodded slightly and said, "You too. Well, see you later."

"Goodbye," he said.

I felt his eyes on me as I exited the elevator, especially on my ass. I walked slowly until I heard the doors close and then exhaled. It was like I'd been holding my breath the entire time. I shook my head, willing myself to get this intriguing man out of my head, but all I could think about was him, his hands, his face, his dark eyes and that fantastic smile. But there was nothing I could do. He was out of the question as far as a romance went. I had a boyfriend of almost four years. We were together, we were a pair. We were going to get married someday.

But I didn't let that stop me from thinking about him. I began to fantasize about Ted and I'd take the elevator as much as possible just so that we might "bump" into each other. However, I didn't see him for almost two weeks. We were in one of the biggest cities in the world and running into someone twice, even if they worked in the same building, was almost an impossibility.

Even so, that didn't keep me from trying. I tried to run into him but to no avail. I'd all but given up when a meeting ran over one day and none of us left the office until after seven. I'd called my boyfriend to explain my lateness. He told me he'd order some Chinese and he'd see me at home.

I was walking to the elevator with several coworkers, chatting about the meeting when I realized I'd left my scarf in my office. I told them I had to run and get it as it was spring and the wind was up. If I didn't wear it, my cheeks would be chapped beyond belief. They told me they'd hold the elevator. I said no thanks, for them to go on, that it was late and we all needed to get home. They smiled and said they'd see me tomorrow.

After I'd retrieved my scarf, I hurried to the elevator and pushed the down button. As I waited, I realized I didn't have much time to get home and do all the things I needed to do: Eat a bite of supper, shower, maybe have a conversation with my boyfriend and then try and get some sleep. I groaned inwardly and had a nice little fantasy about lying on a warm beach somewhere. I wished. That was my ultra goal: A nice beach vacation lying in the warm sun for however long as I wanted. That wasn't going to happen anytime soon.

The elevator doors finally opened and I got on, pushed the button for the lobby and watched as the doors shut. But, instead of going down, the elevator went up.

"What the fuck!" I exclaimed, getting pissed. "Damn it."

I rode the elevator up to the next floor and watched as the doors opened and, much to my astonishment, Ted stepped in. For a second, I almost didn't know what to do. I was floored and my heart started pumping hard.

He stepped on without looking at me, pushed a button, then glanced at me. "Oh, hello! I haven't seen you in quite some time."

I suddenly became tongue-tied, thinking about all the sexual fantasies I'd had since I'd met him that day. I grew embarrassed and didn't know what to say. What do you say to someone you have a sexual crush on? I didn't know so I kept my mouth shut.

"Working late?" he asked, obviously oblivious to my odd behavior.

I nodded and gave him a tight smile.

"Tired?" he asked. "I know I am shattered."

Shattered? I liked how he said that. And his accent was so warm and welcoming. This made me relax so I smiled and said, "Me, too. Exhausted. I can't even think straight."

He nodded, then said, "Would you like to join me for a drink? I'm going for a beer before I head home."

"I can't," I said, thinking about my boyfriend. No, I couldn't do that.

"Oh, sure you could," he said. "One quick drink. Why not?"

I gave him a tight smile and said, "I have a boyfriend."

"That's what I figured," he said. "But it's just a drink, Chloe."

Oh, God! He must have thought I was some sort of idiot or some stupid-full-of-herself-stuck-up-bitch! I cringed with embarrassment and muttered, "No, I didn't think you meant… I mean, I certainly didn't mean—"

"It's okay," he said and laid a hand on my arm gently. "I understand."

And with that, I realized I could trust this guy. He wasn't after me like that. Well, he probably was and if he wasn't, I wanted to be after him. Besides, a drink is just a drink… Yeah. It's just a drink. That would be nice. Why not? So, I said, "Sure. But only one, then I have to get home."

He grinned and said, "I'll have you home at least by midnight."

"Maybe sooner than that," I said. "I am really tired."

We found a bar down the street from our building, then a booth in the back. It was very busy and Ted had to navigate his way through a throng of people to get to the bar where he ordered a beer for himself and a glass of red wine for me.

After he had fought his way back to our table, he set the drinks down and said, "If I'd known it was going to be this busy, we would have gone somewhere else."

I nodded and took a sip of my beer. "Thanks," I said. "So, do you always work this late?"

"Not always," he said. "Just today; it was so harried! I mean, bloody fucking hell, it was one of those days when nothing goes right and… Ahh… Fuck it. Who cares? We're here, having a drink. Life is good again. Cheers."

He held up his glass and clinked it to mine. "Cheers," I muttered and looked around the room, then back at him, taking in his handsome face. "So, what exactly do you do?"

He shrugged. "I'm in management. It's boring. I hate it but the pay is good. What I really want is to move somewhere warm, like Belize or maybe the Cayman Islands, if it weren't so expensive, and buy a little fishing boat and make my living like that. I look great in a tan, by the way."

Wow. He had a similar fantasy to mine. But I guess everyone had a "life at the beach" fantasy, especially when the weather was so cold.

"What do you do?" he asked.

"Sales," I said. "Ditto on the boring part."

He nodded and stared at me, then seemed to blush and look away.

"What is it?"

"You're fucking beautiful," he said. "That's what it is. I have a hard time looking at you."

I blushed and shook my head. "Stop. You're embarrassing me."

He shook his head. "No, I won't stop. Listen," he said and leaned in towards me across the small table. "I won't lie. I've thought about you every single day since we met and wanted to run into you on the elevator or in the lobby or wherever. I'd given up and you suddenly pop up. How's that for fate?"

"Or coincidence," I said quickly.

"No, it's fate or serendipity or whatever," he said softly. He stared into my eyes for a long moment and shook his head slightly. "Fuck me, but I want to fuck you. I'd love to fuck you."

My face burned with his words and his forwardness. Did he just say that? He had and he'd just confirmed my suspicious: We had a strong sexual attraction. But what to do about it? My hands were tied.

"Sorry," he said. "I shouldn't have said that. I can't help myself around you, though. You make me so fucking horny I can't stand it."

I almost cracked up. The accent, the boldness, the slight preposterousness of all of it. But it wasn't funny. It was real.

And he had just spoken my deepest desires. I wanted to fuck him too, and soon. I didn't want to wait. I wanted to get right at it. Life is short and sometimes it just hands you something like this. It was up to me to do something about it. But did I have the guts? Could I go through with it and then deal with the guilt later? I didn't know but I wanted to find out. He was definitely having an effect on me. He was making me want to be young and wild. He was making me want to take that chance. Opportunities rarely came around like this. Why not try it and see where it leads?

I looked him squarely in the face. He glanced up and his eyebrows shot up. He knew something was coming, what, exactly, was anyone's guess. "If you're serious," I said. "Then let's do it."

His mouth dropped. "Really? I was expecting a slap across the cheek for that."

I shook my head. "No, I meant it. Obviously there's an attraction here, so why wait? Why prolong it? What if we never cross paths again and always have to wonder what it would have been like?"

"Wow," he murmured. "You've got it all figured out. I like that."

And I liked his direct approach. I have to admit that's what turned me on most about him. And why not come right out and say what's on your mind sometime? This was my sometime. This was the day I did a little something for myself. That's how I saw it, too, as doing something for me and only for me. All week, even on the weekends, it was about everyone else's needs. It was about doing the laundry or a sales report or reporting to the boss. It was about making time for my boyfriend and buying groceries. It was about all that mundane stuff that, if you really started thinking about, would drive you insane. So I didn't think about it. I put myself on autopilot and I went about my business, getting it done. Today was the day I took a break and did something for myself.

"I don't have all night," I said, wanting him to get the show on the road. "And I don't care what you think. You're up for it, right? So am I. I want it. I've wanted you since the day we met and I am over formalities. I hate chitchat. I don't like innuendo. I want to fuck and I want to fuck you."

"Wow," he said. "Just your words make me hard."

"Then let's get to it," I said.

He nodded, looking around. "Where?"

I looked around the bar then thought about the bathroom. No, too dirty and too small. I couldn't take him back home and I didn't know how far away his apartment was. Where could we fuck?

"We'll figure it out," I said and took off my glasses, slipping them into my purse. I noticed he was watching me, so I said, "I just need them mostly for reading. And working on the computer."

He nodded that he understood.

I stood, holding out my hand. "Let's go. Ready?"

"Abso-fucking-lutely," he muttered and grabbed my hand. I allowed him to pull us through the crowd, out the door and down the street and then into an alley. I'd never had sex outside, let alone in a public place. I didn't care though. I just wanted him and I wanted him, like, yesterday. So, whatever. I'd make whatever concessions I had to as long as I got him. And soon.

Once we were there, he grinned, looked around to make sure no one was around, then literally threw me up against the brick wall. I moaned as his lips overtook mine, sucking them into his mouth and eating at me. It was like this surge of energy, of electricity, was coursing through our bodies and we were fusing together. He ate at my mouth, thrusting his tongue into my mouth and I sucked on it while I grabbed at his cock, which was hard and quite large. I rubbed it through his pants as we sucked face and his hand went up my shirt and squeezed my breast hard, then he pulled back, ripped my shirt open and forced his face into my shirt and his mouth beneath my bra. Once his mouth grabbed onto my erect nipple, I screamed with ecstasy. It felt so good and I hadn't felt this sort of passion in at least a few years.

"Fuck me," I said and moved my hands to his shoulders, grabbing onto him. "I am so wet now."

He slipped his hand up my skirt and rubbed my pussy. "You are," he breathed. "You're so wet."

I grabbed his face and kissed him again, sucking at his mouth. "Please," I begged. "Fuck me!"

He pulled my panties off and then rammed his hard and throbbing cock into my wet, willing and wanting pussy. I shuddered at how good it felt, that skin on skin contact, that pussy and cock union.

I wrapped my legs around his waist and began to ride him. *Ahh*, it felt so good and it was so easy to get my groove on. Because I was so turned on, I came without even trying. The orgasm ripped through my body and came out in an intense moan from my throat. *Uhhgh*! I moaned with it, shook with it and then felt him coming and coming hard. I hung on until he finished with a shudder and a moan. He gave me one good, last thrust and then we kissed as we came down from the cloud of good feeling.

"Mmmm..." he moaned and nuzzled my neck. "That was a good fuck."

"Yes," I said and kissed his cheek, then pulled away. "I have to get home."

"I'll walk you," he said.

"No, I'll take a cab," I replied and adjusted my skirt and top. I looked around for my panties, saw them on the nasty ground and then noticed a trash can. I went over, picked them up and tossed them into the garbage. He watched me, bemused.

"I guess that's one way to get rid of the evidence," he said.

"It is," I said and winked at him. "Listen, this is the way it's going to go down. Come to my office tomorrow at seven. I'll be ready."

He stared at me and grinned. "So, you want some more?"

"I do," I said. "Don't be late."

I gave him one last quick kiss then went home, said hello to my boyfriend, took a quick shower and slept like a baby.

௸

The next day, at the end of the day, Ted came into my office without a word. I didn't have anything to say, either.

We stared at each other. This was it. Could I do it again? I'd done it last night. I'd made my excuses to my boyfriend about another late meeting. I'd waited all day, till the end of the day, for this. And I wanted it. But I was nervous. Would it be as good as it had been previously? *Fuck it.* I had to find out so I plunged in before I chickened out. I was ready. My glasses were off, my skin was tingling. I was getting wet just thinking about what we were about to do. It was *time*.

I leaned over and pressed my mouth against his, breathing in his smell, his skin, him. He gasped a little and grabbed my face, holding me tight, like he was never going to let me go. I allowed it for a few seconds, then pushed him back. None of that just yet. I wanted to get down to business. So, I got down to it by getting down on my knees.

Before I unzipped his pants, I glanced up at him and couldn't help but smile at the look of surprise and joy on his face. He couldn't believe his luck. Well, neither could I.

Once his pants were unzipped, I pulled out his cock, then looked up at him and began to stroke it. He stared down at me and I could see the lust in his eyes. I licked my lips, then slide my tongue across the tip before taking it into my mouth. He moaned loudly and exhaled sharply as I began to suck his cock, sucking so hard, I was sure he'd explode in my mouth. And I wanted him, too. I didn't normally do things like this with my boyfriend but with him, I wanted to do it, I wanted to be dirty.

I could tell me was about to come and I could tell he had some other things on his mind. I pulled back and stared up at him, then gave his cock one last hard suck.

"Come on, love," he said and grabbed me up under the arms and turned me around so that my ass was in front of him and I was facing my desk. He ran his hands up and down my ass, up and down my legs, then began to plant small kisses onto the backs of my thighs while his hand made its way under my skirt and into my panties. Ahhh… It felt so good. He began to rub my pussy with deep, long strokes. I moved with his hand and rubbed against it, feeling the good, hard pressure on my clit.

Without a word, he pushed my skirt up and over my ass and then pulled my legs apart, burying his face into my pussy. I hissed with passion and widened my stance, glad I'd left my stilettos on so I could have some height. And then he began to eat at me, sucking at my pussy, before he found my clit, which he gave several long, flat-tongued licks to before sucking at it. I let out a little wail as the orgasm hit me, took me over and sent me clawing at the desk, knocking my phone and pencil holder off. I began to ride his face, extending the orgasm and rode it out until there was nothing left.

He turned me around.

I greeted him with open arms, pulling him into me and taking off his jacket and shirt as I locked my lips to his. I ran my hands up and down his smooth, muscled torso, then leaned over and licked and nibbled at his nipples. He pulled me back up and kissed me hard while unbuttoning my shirt and I helped him to slip it off my back. Then he unsnapped my bra and grabbed my tits. He squeezed them together then bent over and gave the nipples, which were already hard and tender, several long licks until I was almost writhing with lust.

I couldn't take much more. I wanted his cock in me and I wanted it fucking me. I grabbed onto it, pushing his pants off with my legs and lay back on the desk, opening my legs up wide for him. He climbed onto the desk and mounted me, pushing his hard, throbbing member deep into my cunt. I moaned when he was all the way in. and then we fucked. We fucked hard. I grabbed onto his ass, pushing him as deeply as he could go inside and sucked on his neck. Ummm… It felt so good, so dirty and slightly nasty. I could not get enough.

"I'm gonna come," he moaned.

"Shh," I whispered into his ear, then licked it. "Slow down. Let me have more."

He nodded and backed himself off the orgasm. I began to fuck him, moving my pussy up and down his cock, squeezing it into me and riding it for all it was worth. It wasn't long before I found my groove and felt the orgasm take over. I moaned and threw my head back just as it hit me and he started pumping into me as soon as I began to come.

Just as he came, he pulled out and shot his hot semen all over my stomach. I gyrated with it, moving this way and that as it splashed all over me, loving the sticky and hot cum. He leaned over and kissed me hard, pressing his mouth onto mine. I kissed back, unable to control myself, and knew, just knew I was going to get what I wanted. And I wanted more.

ɷ

At the end of the day, it became about the sex. Just the sex. Sure, Ted would bring me little trinkets from time to time—flowers, delicious dark chocolates and even a pair of Tiffany earrings once. But I didn't care about any of that. It was just about the sex. I wanted him, his cock, and that's all.

He did mention me leaving my boyfriend for him once and I stopped him right there. There would be no talk of that. What we did was between us and it was unfair to bring my boyfriend into it.

And, yes, I did feel some guilt about doing it. But I put that out of my mind. I knew this wouldn't last and I wasn't doing it to hurt anyone. I was doing it out of sheer lust and boredom with my life. I'd never had sex that good and it was something I needed. It was the ray of sunshine in my otherwise drab days. It was what I thought about when I did something I loathed, like cleaning the bathtub or poring over a sales report. It was my time and I was taking my time.

Our routine was simple. I'd make arrangements to meet him, usually after seven. He'd come down the elevator, get off, find me and we'd fuck. We fucked all over my floor, too, even on my bosses' desk. It was fun and it was lively and it was everything I'd ever fantasized about.

He loved to give it to me from behind. This one time, he turned me over, pushed open my legs and shoved his hard cock into me. I began to move with him until I felt his finger slide down between the cheeks of my ass. Without hesitation, he kept sliding until he found the entrance and then he slipped the finger in as he fucked me. Oh, *fuck*, that felt good! I gritted my teeth and pushed back against him as he gave it to me. I rose up and grabbed his other hand, placing it on my breast. I put my hand between my legs, on my clit, and had all of the major erotic areas covered. It was a fuck fest that night. He kept pumping into me and fucking me while fingering me. I came so hard I thought I might pass out.

He also loved to eat me out. He loved to dive in and suck and lick at my pussy until it was hot and wet. His skin would be slightly rough from his five-o'clock shadow and I loved to rub my soft skin onto it and get that scratchy, yet good feeling. Then I'd lick his lips softly until I elicited a deep moan from him and he'd take over.

I loved it when he took over. Some days, without a word, he'd come into my office, shut the door and turn out all the lights. Then he'd grab me, throw me up against the wall and take me, fucking me silly until I was begging him for more.

We wore each other out. I never wanted it to end. But all good things eventually come to an end and so did our sexual relationship. He got transferred to another city and I stayed behind. He begged me to leave with him, on his hands and knees, no less, but I refused. I didn't want to uproot my life for anyone and I knew that while I did have feelings for him, I was still in love with my boyfriend. I also knew he could be easily replaced. I never considered myself a cheater, but I knew that door had been opened and where I took it was at my discretion.

But I do glance at my watch or at the clock at seven every night. Wherever I am, I check the time and I think of him and I think about how, at the end of the day, we'd given each other much, much pleasure. It's a fond memory I'd love to relive. But for now, that's all it was.

On the Same Page

The pay was good; the sex was even better. No. I wasn't getting paid for having sex with my boss. I was getting paid for being his assistant. The sex was just an added bonus. In fact, I would have paid him to have sex with me.

Yeah, he was that good.

It didn't start out like that, though. I disliked him at first sight even though he had to be one of the best looking men I'd ever laid eyes on. But looks can be deceiving and he looked *good*. However, he was overly obsessive and somewhat rude. He was tall. Handsome. I liked his hands, which were wide and strong looking. But him? As a person? I didn't like him. He was arrogant. He was one of those super-successful businessmen who knew he was the shit. He had it all—the penthouse in the expensive neighborhood, the driver who rode him around in a sleek black European car, the maids, the underlings, the expensive watches, the tailored suits. He had all the trappings of success. He had everything. Everything but me, that is.

I wouldn't let him have me. Well, not at first, at least. We weren't on the same page, as they say. I was in a subservient position, one I didn't like finding myself in and one that he wouldn't let me forget. I had some resentment because of it. I guess it came out and he treated me in kind.

"You can be such a bitch, Chloe," he told me one day. "Why are you such a bitch?"

"Because I don't like you," I told him, just to irritate him. He wanted everyone to like him though he, himself, was one of the hardest people in the world to get along with.

But, as I was saying, at that time I didn't really like him that much, especially not in that way. But after a while? Oh, yes, I did, very much so though I couldn't let on like I did. I kept up the bitchy façade and he tried his best to please me; sexually, I mean. The thought of he and I having wild sex never left me, even when I went home on Saturday nights. I would think of him all week, the lust building in me as the days went by. On Mondays I could contain it. On Tuesdays I was getting antsy. On Wednesdays I was nearly out of my mind. On Thursdays I was giving my vibrator a run for its money. On Fridays I was back to containing myself but just barely. But by the time I saw him on Saturday mornings, it was hard to hold myself off of him. Even so, it took us a while to warm up to each other.

But for the longest time I didn't let him know my feelings. I didn't want him to know I wanted him. Every girl wanted him. Every woman wanted to be his plaything, to be his girlfriend, to be his wife. He was wanted by many, many women. I didn't want to seem like one of those girls and it came out in bitchy behavior.

It's just that he drove me crazy with all his little obsessions. This led to me smarting off about something, how his hair looked like it needed a little trimming or how a proposal seemed a little over-worded. Things like this drove him crazy and sometimes he spanked me for my insubordination. He did it to emphasize that I was a bad girl who needed to be put in her place. Well, that much was obvious.

Before that, though, there was Ted. Ted was the man I'd had an affair with prior to meeting Mr. OCD Businessman. Ted was the man I had previously longed for and wished I hadn't let get away. But my boyfriend, and my guilt about having an actual affair, got in the way. I couldn't leave my boyfriend for him, that much was easy to figure out. But what I really didn't want to give up was my security. I loved having my comfortable life. I loved my job and, yes, even though he was no Ted, I loved my boyfriend.

However, he began to *bore* me after Ted. I couldn't stand to be around him. The breakup was rather quick. I just withdrew and started bitching about everything in sight. Soon enough, he got the hint and packed up and left one day while I was at work. The note on the kitchen counter? It was simple and effectual: *I'm sick of it. You can have it.*

He may have given me my freedom but he also left me with an expensive lease on our one-bedroom mid-town apartment. The lease wasn't up for months. I was stuck with it. If I wanted out of it, I'd have to pay a lot of money I simply didn't have. I made good money, but not enough to cover all of my expenses and my rent. Of course, I could have gotten a cheaper apartment. I could have moved to another part of the city. But I didn't want to. I loved my neighborhood and I loved my apartment. It was the apartment all young women want when they move to the big city. It was in an older building, had unique characteristics and, oddly enough, had been a steal at the time we signed the lease. It was the deal of a lifetime. However, it still took two incomes to cover it. I couldn't afford it on my salary alone. But to let it go without a fight? No. I couldn't. I just *couldn't.* I knew I was hanging on to the ideal, even if it was to my detriment.

I was in a pickle. But at least now I was free to call Ted. However, something inside of me just wouldn't let me. I don't know if I subconsciously knew he wasn't the one for me or that I was kinda digging having all this freedom. I'd been in a relationship most of my adult life and the thought of diving right back in, even though the sex was that hot, was unappealing.

Regardless, there was still the issue of my rent. It was an astronomical amount to pay and, with my boyfriend out of the picture and no longer helping, I was going broke fast. It was inevitable that I had to start dipping into my savings just to cover it. After a few months of this, and the new of living alone had worn off, I realized that I was going to have to do something about my situation. I had to get a raise. I approached my boss with it one morning.

"Come in," she said and motioned me into her spacious corner office. She smiled at me and asked, "How are you, Chloe?"

I smiled back. She and I were on good terms and worked well together. She was nice and I hoped the fact that she liked me would reward me with some extra cash. So, I said, "I'm fine, Alexis. And you?"

"Couldn't be better," she replied. "What can I do for you?"

I sat down in one of the two chairs in front of her desk. "Listen, I know you are strapped for time so I am just going to cut to the chase. I need a raise. Badly."

She stared at me with a sight look of shock combined with sadness. "I'm sorry, Chloe, but I can't swing it. There's simply no room in the budget for pay increases. You know yourself there have been cutbacks."

I nodded. I knew this. It was true. I knew I was very lucky to have my job but the pay just wasn't cutting it. If she couldn't help me, I would have to find a better paying job and, let's just say, finding a better paying job in this economy was an impossibility. And even then I'd probably still have to move once the lease was up on my apartment.

She stared at me sadly and said, "I wish I could help."

"Me too," I said and took off my glasses then rubbed my eyes. What a mess I had gotten myself into with Ted. I should have run from him. But the sex had been so good, so great. Yeah, it was worth it. But soon, if things didn't change monetarily, it wouldn't matter. I couldn't live on a memory.

She sighed and said, "Listen I heard something through the grapevine and I am going to preface this by saying, I don't like my employees moonlighting."

I sat up. What was she talking about?

"There is someone who is looking for a person to assist them on the weekends," she said.

"Okay," I said, nodding.

"I just hate this," she said. "I don't want you to do this, but it might be a good option. Bottom line: Sven Aslin is looking for an assistant. Just for the weekends. I heard about it over lunch the other day."

"Sven Aslin?" I asked, mouth agape. He was, like, one of the biggest big shots in the city. He was, like, rich. He was very well respected by his peers but to others he was a real asshole. I'd seen his pictures in the papers, always with a big-boobed blonde hanging on his arm. If that was any indicator of what he was like, that meant he was narcissistic, and, apparently, very superficial.

"Yes," she said and wrote something down on a piece of paper. "His current assistant used to work for me a few years ago. She and I ran into each other at lunch, like I said." She leaned over and handed me the piece of paper. "Here's her number."

I took it and stared at it.

"She just got married and can't work on the weekends for him anymore," she said. "Call her. It might be a good option for you until, perhaps, we can do something here."

I nodded. I didn't like the idea of working on the weekends that was for sure. When would I do my laundry? Clean my apartment? Grocery shop? And what about working out? Those two days off were the only days I actually got to the gym. Fuck! Life was so hard sometimes. But I'd brought this on myself by getting some sex on the side. It was my fault and I should have not done it. Damn Ted anyway.

"Thank you," I said and stood. "I'll call her on my lunch hour."

"Chloe," she said before I left the room. "Be careful. I've heard quite a lot about Sven. He can be a handful."

I nodded. It wasn't him I was worried about. I was worried about me.

℔

His assistant set up an interview for eight o'clock that evening. Good thing, too, as I had to work late and his offices were within walking distance from my building. I grabbed a quick bite to eat on my way over, stuffing a slice of pepperoni pizza in my mouth and sipping on a soda. Of course, some of the grease from the pepperoni dripped onto my shirt, so I went into the bathroom in the lobby and tried to dab it off. The water only made it worse. *Great.* I looked a wreck. My hair was disheveled. My eyes were tired. My skirt was wrinkled and, now, my shirt was greasy. I should have just gone home and said to hell with it.

Again, I should have just moved. I should have tried to find a way out of that apartment. But it was almost a matter of pride for me at that point. I had to do this. I had to make it work. I had to prove to myself that I could do this without a man. I couldn't fail.

His secretary, who was obviously pissed off that she had to work over for me, gave me a terse smile then showed me into his spacious office and then shut the door behind her. The room was empty and I had time to look around at the super-expensive Herman Miller desk and the Eames chairs and the modern, tufted leather sofa. I sat down in one of the two chairs in front of the desk and glanced around the room. Nice. Very, very nice. And the taste was exquisite, of course.

There was very little clutter and the books and knickknacks on the shelves were placed *just so*. Typical OCD personality. I didn't know if I was up for this or not.

As I looked around the room, I began to wonder what kind of man was this guy, really? Was the mid-century décor and super-neat surroundings just a product of his decorator? Or was he really into this stuff? I didn't know but I did appreciate it. The modern art on the walls, one of which looked like a real Warhol, really intrigued me. Really? Seriously? This guy had to have some major cash.

"Sorry to keep you waiting," someone said behind me.

I turned to see him walking quickly and with purpose into the room with his hand extended towards me. I rose out of my chair and held out my hand. He gave me a hasty shake then went behind his desk, sat down and loosened his tie.

"So," he said. "You are Chloe?"

"I am," I said and sat back down.

"Sven Aslin," he said. "You know of me? Yes?"

I stared at him. Did I detect a slight Swedish accent? I think I did. "Are you Swedish?" I asked. I mean, I knew he was. I just didn't expect the slight accent. It was nice, though. I liked it.

"I am," he said. "From Sweden. But I have lived in America since I was a teenage boy. My mother is American. She and I came over here after my parents' divorce."

"Oh," I said.

"To cut to the chase," he said and leaned back in his chair, staring at me. "I am looking for someone to work with me on the weekends. The job would involve some clerical duties, some light shopping, perhaps, and accompanying me on business trips to tend to my needs. How are you on the computer?"

"Fine," I said. "I know the basics, of course. PowerPoint, Word, Excel, things like that."

He nodded. "Good, that is all I require, really." He sighed. "I am not an easy man to work for, Chloe. I demand quite a lot out of my assistants. I will require a lot out of you. If you fuck up on me, I will fire you on the spot. If you do not do as I request, I will fire you."

My face burned a little with his words. He was a hard-ass. I hadn't expected that of him. He was handsome with dark blonde hair that was cut short. Oh, God, he was very handsome. His eyes were a light blue and his skin looked fresh and tanned, as if he'd just come back from a Bahamas beach vacation. I liked him well enough. Well as far as looks went anyway but I could tell this man didn't pull any punches and he certainly didn't take any shit.

"My assistant refused to work for me on the weekends anymore," he said. "She threatened to quit. But she just got married and I like her. Good assistants are hard to find so I could not fire her. I decided to compromise instead."

I supposed that was nice of him. I didn't really know for sure because she might have been the only person who could stand to work with him. I could tell he was going to be very, very demanding.

"So," I said. "You have an assistant and a secretary?"

"Yes," he said. "My secretary handles a lot of things that happen here in this office and my assistant handles things that happen out of the office and helps also on a more personal level. I need a lot of help," he added with a slight chuckle.

You could say that, I thought sarcastically to myself. But I kept my mouth shut. I needed this job. I couldn't fuck it up. I could put up with him. I could do what he wanted, collect my pay and go on with my life. And probably still end up moving to another, cheaper apartment. Why didn't I just go ahead and give in and save myself the trouble? And I knew that Sven was going to be trouble. A lot of trouble.

"I can't stand it anymore," he said suddenly. "What the fuck is that on your shirt?"

I jerked a little at his words then looked down at the grease stain and said, "Pizza. Sorry. I didn't have time to change before I came over."

"Are you working late every day?" he asked, staring at the stain.

I shook my head. "No, not every day. Just a few times a month. Sales meetings, mostly, with foreign clients."

He nodded that he understood. "I can't have *that.* It's bothering me. I can't stand untidiness or uncleanness. I am a little OCD that way. You will have to change shirts."

"Right now?" I asked, my eyes nearly popping out of my skull.

He nodded quickly, looking around. Then he got up, went to a door I hadn't noticed and pulled out a freshly dry-cleaned shirt from the closet. He tore the plastic off, pulled it off the rack and handed it to me. "Go into the bathroom and change into that."

I stared at him, then at the shirt. He was kidding, right? I looked more closely at him. He was not kidding. Fuck! He was going to be such an asshole! I was in for it, all because I had to have an affair with the best looking Englishman around. It was my fault but it was still painful.

"Fine," I said and got up and went into the bathroom, took off my glasses and threw them on the sink then changed into the shirt. Sven was a big man so the shirt completely dwarfed my petite frame. I groaned and stared at myself in the mirror. Due to reduced circumstances, I had stopped coloring my hair the nice, honey-blonde it had been and the roots were coming out to the natural brunette it was. Soon, I'd be totally brunette again. It wasn't a bad change, though. The darker hair contrasted well with my dark blue eyes. My face was pretty; I'd even been told I was beautiful on occasion, but I looked tired, like I needed a long vacation.

I thought about my happy place, the Cayman Islands, and went there in my mind for a minute, imagining myself on the beach staring at the pretty waves of the ocean.

I opened my eyes and stared at my glasses on the sink and then back at myself in the mirror. What was I doing? Could I do this? It was going to be such a pain in the ass. I stood there for a moment or two contemplating what I was going to do. I was *this close* to putting my shirt back on and walking out. But I couldn't.

I shook myself out of my contemplation, grabbed my glasses, put them back on and turned to the door, drawing in my breath and preparing myself. I opened the door and went back out. I exhaled loudly, hating that I'd been forced into this situation. But I had no other alternative. I needed the money and if that meant I had to put up with Sven, then that's what it meant.

He nodded with approval, and what seemed like a little relief, at the shirt and said, "I have checked all your references and you come highly recommended. Can you start this Saturday?"

"Of course," I said.

"Wonderful," he said and wrote something down on a piece of paper and handed it to me. "That is my home address."

I glanced at the paper and checked out his address. He had an apartment in one of the most exclusive neighborhoods in the city. Of course. Why wouldn't he?

He said, "We will meet there and sometimes we will meet here. It depends on what I have going on during the week. Be punctual, never late. If you are late, I will fire you on the spot."

I didn't respond but I did take note.

"Also, we will work through our lunches," he said and moved the pencil holder on his desk slightly to the left. As he did so, he said, "And I expect perfection. I know that you will not always be able to achieve it but you must make the effort. I don't like incompetence." He stared at the pencil holder, ascertained that it was in the correct position, then slightly moved his keyboard to the left. "If you are not nearly perfect, you will be fired on the spot. We must work together, as a team. If we don't get along well enough, you will be fired. Understood?"

Hard. Ass. Control. Freak. This was the main reason why I disliked working for super-rich, super-successful people. To get to their level, they had to be a little off their rocker and totally egomaniacal. It didn't work any other way. And he was very much an egomaniac and a little off, too. I mean, he was taking time to work out the exact placement of his pencil holder and keyboard. I realized the office was all his. He'd probably designed it down to the last detail and arranged everything *just so*. I'd be willing to bet the cleaning lady got her ass chewed if he found anything out of place.

Poor woman. Poor me.

"So, Saturday," he said and clapped his hands together. "Welcome onboard, Chloe. We will spend many hours working."

Oh. Joy.

&

Well, at least the pay was excellent. That was one good thing. It would, basically, pay for the rent on my apartment and leave me some left over for the little luxuries in life like soap and coffee. I almost rolled my eyes. I never knew it would be this hard for a single woman to make it in the city.

Maybe I should have just moved. No, I should have just moved, told my landlord I didn't have any money and said goodbye. I could have sublet the apartment or at least have gotten a roommate. But that wasn't an option yet, just not yet. I was holding on, praying I could do this on my own. This job was the only option I had.

Yes, Sven drove me crazy. The job was tough and it took almost every spare hour I had on the weekends. I'd get up at seven and either meet him at his totally fabulous and jealousy-inducing penthouse apartment or at his offices. From there, it was non-stop work and he was always hovering around me, checking everything I did to see if I misspelled something on a proposal or to see if I'd put in the right numbers on a spreadsheet. He'd ask a thousand times if I'd gotten in touch with this business associate or that one. He'd ask over and over if I remembered his dry cleaning if his maid was out of town. He really needed *that* particular shirt or *that* particular suit. Did I get it? Was it cleaned? Was it cleaned properly? Be sure to place them in the closet properly, otherwise it would get wrinkled. He couldn't have it wrinkled. Wrinkles would drive him crazy.

But not as crazy as he drove me.

He'd ask if I could *make sure* to schedule his dinner reservations at eight and then he'd ask me to confirm this. Then he'd remind me a thousand times to be sure I had made the reservations in the first place. Then he'd make me call the restaurant to make sure they had not screwed up his dinner reservations. *They're at eight, right? Eight on the nose. Eight? Right? At eight? Tell me, are they at eight? Have they been scheduled? At eight?*

It was more than a bit maddening.

He had to have me around at all times, too. I even had to go with him while he played tennis and stand to the side just in case he wanted to dictate some correspondence. "Text that asshole Balder! Tell him that we have to meet Monday morning or it's off! At eight!" he'd yell out of the blue and I'd text like crazy as he and his tennis instructor fought it out on the court: "Balder, Mon@8orOff!"

He just never stopped working. He never took any time off. Never. I repeat: *Never.* How he kept from having a major coronary was beyond me. I went to the ladies room one afternoon and was freshening up my makeup when he had the fucking nerve to pound on the door, asking me what I was doing, telling me if I wasn't sick that it was time to get back to work! I didn't see how he kept anyone working for him. He worked me like a dog. I was paid well but I earned every last cent. I now knew why he was so reluctant to lose his assistant and that's because he'd never be able to get another one.

Not only that, my clothing, hair and nails had to be immaculate at all times. I had assumed that because we were working on the weekends I could dress down. Not so. The first day I showed up in jeans and wedges, he sent me right back home to change into business attire.

Of course, he dressed more casually on the weekends. Well, at least as casually as someone like him could. He'd occasionally wear his tennis whites or some khakis what were so starched they looked almost wooden. Sometimes he'd wear some black slacks with a blue silk button down shirt and no tie. (This was causal to him.) But me? No. It was skirts and heels. Not only did I get to dress up for my job during the week, I got to dress up on the weekends. Actually, I had to dress more nicely for my weekend job than I did for my normal job. Yea! And I had to stay neat as a pin, too, all fresh and clean. No stains, either. If I spilled anything on myself, it was back home to change. So, whenever I ate lunch, I began to hold the food away from me so I wouldn't spill anything on my clothes because, if I did, I had to take a trip home to change. After a while, I stopped ordering anything that might drip or spill. And I always sipped my drinks through a straw. Heaven forbid if I splashed soda on my skirt!

The only saving grace was my baggy sweats and oversized t-shirts I'd fall into once I got home at night.

By Sunday night, I would be so exhausted I usually fell asleep on my couch. I'd dream of my happy place, the beach, and pray to win the lottery. But I never played the lottery, mostly because I was so tired I would forgot to pick a ticket up.

It was maddening. Sven was so obsessive compulsive I wondered how he even functioned. He was always checking and making sure things on his desk were in perfect alignment. Not a minute passed by that he wasn't on his computer or on the phone, always, always conducting some sort of business.

If we weren't at his apartment or at his offices, we were in his chauffeur driven car traveling across the city. And, even then, it was about work. I was either on my phone making calls or checking emails or I was on the computer typing something all while listening him yammer on his phone in Swedish.

Needless to say, I took a lot of aspirin during that time. He got on my nerves so badly, it took everything I had not to tell him to fuck off.

This went on for six months. By that time, I had begun to look for cheaper apartments. I didn't care about the stainless steel appliances or the subway tiles in the bath or the perfectly worn wood floors anymore. Yes, my apartment was fantastic but it was not worth this. Nothing was.

One Saturday night we were, as usual, burning the midnight oil at his office. He'd poured us each a glass of red wine as a treat for working late. One thing about him, he loved his wine and he only drank the best, which was fine by me. I liked wine, too, though I wasn't quite as enthusiastic about it as he was. So, I sipped mine as I pounded out a letter to someone as he dictated. He walked the floor behind me, sprouting off what needed to be said and sipped his wine as he did so.

As I typed, I'd pick up my glass, take a sip then set it back down close to the edge of the table each time so I could reach it more easily. This, of course, drove him crazy and he'd take the glass and move it more in the center of the table. He did stuff like this all the time and I didn't even realize he was doing it as I'd been so accustomed to putting up with it.

But after about the third time, it suddenly dawned on me what he was doing. I glanced at the clock on the wall and saw that it was close to eleven at night. This pissed me off. Here I was typing my brains out and he was pulling his usual OCD shit with me. A flash of anger spread through my body. I lit up with it and felt my heart start to beat rapidly. I had had it. This was *it*. I should be home, sleeping or at least watching some TV. But, no, I was there with this lunatic. I decided then and there that no apartment was worth this torment and that I was moving. I was *done*.

He finally stopped dictating and told me to finish the letter off and yadda yadda yadda. I did so, then picked up my wine and took a small sip. Then I set it back down on the edge of the table. Without thought, he picked the glass up and placed it towards the center. I picked it up, moved it back to the edge and turned to him. He eyed me. I eyed him back and then I was just so sick of it. Seriously, I was sick of it. He and I stared each other down. He wanted to leap and move the glass but I had other things in mind. *What is she going to do?* he seemed to wonder.

I was going to fuck with him.

So, I tapped the stem of the glass lightly with my pen—*clink, clink, clink*—until it fell off the edge of the table and onto the floor. Wine spilled everywhere. There was so much I wondered if it'd been booby-trapped or something. I'd never seen such a mess and, for an instant, I regretted my actions.

He eyed the spilled wine, then turned to me. In a second he was on me and had me pulled up by my wrists. "You did that on purpose!"

I nodded. "Yeah, so what? You gonna fire me?"

He eyed me then thrust me away from him, going into the bathroom then returning with two washcloths, one wet and one dry. He blotted the wine with the dry one then rubbed the wet washcloth across the stain. I waited with anticipation to see what he was going to do to me. He continued to clean the stain, getting most of it up, then took the washcloths into the bathroom, came back out and turned to me.

"You can go now," he said.

I nodded. I thought that's how this would all end. Fine. Whatever. I grabbed my bag and started out the door when he threw up his hand. I halted and turned to him. "Yes?"

"The cost of cleaning the rug will come out of your pay," he said.

"*What?*" I growled under my breath but didn't say a word. *Fine.*

"And, just so you know, I will not be giving you a recommendation."

"I don't need your fucking recommendation," I said. "I already have a job. I'm just doing this for extra money, that's all."

He nodded. "And what if I called your boss, who recommended me to you? She is one of my business associates and I do not believe she would like your behavior."

"Are you threatening me?" I asked. "Because that sort of sounded like a threat."

"No threat," he said. "I do not do that. If I want to do something, I do something with no threat. That is the way I operate."

He was such an asshole. He had such power and control it killed me, probably because I felt so out of control since I'd met Ted, had my affair and broken up with my boyfriend.

Without thought of consequence, I threw my bag down, stomped over to him and slapped him. Just like that. His head went to the side then came back to center so that his eyes were throwing daggers at me. I glared back at him, daring him to do something about it. Wanting him to do something about it. And, much to my surprise, he did.

He grabbed my arm and pulled me down with him into a chair so that my body was across his lap and my ass was in the air. Then he pushed my skirt up and he gave me a good, hard slap right across my ass.

Oh, no, he didn't. Oh, yes. He did.

Before I could protest, he gave me another hard slap and another. I screamed as his hand slapped my ass each time. He was spanking me like I'd been disobedient and very naughty and that *really* pissed me off. I did try to wriggle out of his lap and gain some of my dignity back but he held me tight, not letting me move. Then he pretty much started to beat my ass.

Once it was over, he shoved me out of his lap and I teetered a little, trying to gain my balance. We stared at each other and I felt the sting on my butt. But then I realized something. He'd stepped out of line with me, *way* out of line. He had lost some of his precious control. And I had gained some. As he stared back, he realized it too and I could see regret begin to stamp itself over his face. It came out in ugly red blotches.

Well, well, well.

Without a word, I pushed my skirt down and picked up my bag again. I turned to leave and gave my ass a little wiggle before disappearing out the door.

☙

"I would like to apologize," he said, entering my apartment. "I was out of line."

I had almost fallen over when the doorbell had rung an hour after I'd gotten home. I'd just stepped out of the shower and had thrown on my old, baggy pair of sweats and a white t-shirt. My feet were bare and my hair was still wet. He eyed me and I could tell that my sloppy appearance was bothering him. Good. That's what he needed.

However, strangely enough I was glad to see him. I don't know why but something about the way he took control of me and spanked me like that really turned me on. I would never admit it to him, but it did. I had a hard time admitting it to myself but it was true.

"I apologize," he said and glanced around the room, seeming to breathe a sigh of relief that it was tidy, clean and organized. I could tell he liked my more modern taste in furniture and appreciated the expensive details of the apartment like the crown molding and the gas fireplace with the marble surround.

"Hmmm," I said, thinking it over. It was good that he was apologizing. But I wasn't about to let him know that.

"So, do you accept my apology?" he asked. "Can we move forward?"

"Maybe," I said, turning to him. "However, I think you're just afraid of what I might tell other people." I smiled at him, loving the fact that I had him by the balls.

"Perhaps," he said. "How much is this going to cost me?"

I thought about that. Yeah. I was certainly in the power position now.

"Name your amount," he said, as if he were prepared to whip out his checkbook and write it out.

I didn't answer. Mainly because I had other things in mind.

"Chloe?" he said. "Are we on the same page?"

He always asked me that. "Are we on the same page, Chloe?" Oh, it drove me mad. It was a business cliché I disliked. Everyone overused it but none more than him. "Chloe, are we on same page?" "Let's get on the same page here." "Chloe, I would like to be on the same page with you." "Tell me we're on the same page!" Just to shut him up, I'd eventually say, "Yes, Sven, we are on the same page."

But, no, weren't on the same page where this matter was concerned.

"Chloe," he said. "Tell me how much."

I didn't want his money. I wanted something else from him.

"I'll tell you what I want," I said and went over and stood behind the sofa. I pulled off my sweats and kicked them to the side, then bent over the couch, my naked ass— still a little red from the spanking—in the air, inviting him to do something about it. Was I doing this? Really? Was I offering myself to him? Asking for another spanking? I was. Hey, I hadn't been laid in a while and I'd never really been spanked. It was new to me and I liked it. I wanted a little more where that came from. And, really, where could you find a man that knew how to do that in this city? They were a rarity and he was going to do what I wanted him to do. It was that simple.

I didn't even realize I could be like that, offering myself like that, that I could do something like that, which was a little slutty. But that was okay. Something inside of me guided me to this. Maybe it was because I was horny and needed to get laid, like an itch must be scratched. Maybe I was just looking for a connection, like the connection I'd felt with Ted. Sure, I was lonely and I was a little naughty but there was something about Sven that brought it out in me. A need had been awakened and I had to just go with it.

Besides, I loved sex. And it had been a while.

He didn't move. I stood up and raised one eyebrow at him. He stared at me, at my tight ass and then at my face. We locked eyes and right then we both knew what we wanted from the other. We wanted to move on from this nasty little situation. He knew now where I wanted to take it. *But where would he take it?* Sure, he'd just wanted to buy me off. But I wasn't that easy. He should have known that.

He took a deep breath and came up behind me, grabbed my ass with both hands and squeezed the cheeks. Then he pushed my head down until I was bent over the couch. Then I heard him taking off his belt. Wait a second! I didn't want that! I just wanted a spanking. But before I could protest, he gave me a good hard lash with the belt. *Whack!* I shuddered. It burned. And then I gasped.

"I will not play with you," he said. "I will not."

Then what did he intend to do? I realized I was quite under his control then and very, very vulnerable. Had I pushed him too far? What was he going to do? And when? How long did I have to wait?

The belt came down on my ass hard again. This time it hurt worse. I couldn't move or think straight. I just stood there and let him whip me. For a second I thought I should run but then I thought I should stay and see where this would lead. Yeah, I was totally turned on.

"Umm," he said, pausing, and rubbed my ass cheeks. "Tight. Is your pussy as tight as your ass?"

Wow. Ummm… Ow. My ass hurt a little and gave slight throbs occasionally, but his words overrode any pain I felt from the belt. I hadn't expected that from him. *Pussy?*

I'd never, in a million years, expected that word to come out of his mouth. But it was nice that it had. He was a little dirty. I liked that and his words turned me on. They were gruff. I liked that. But I didn't know if my pussy was as tight as my ass. I guessed so. Who asks a question like that? How do you respond to something like that? However, I pretended to shrug it off.

He leaned in over me and pressed his face close to my ear and whispered, "I am a man, Chloe. What if I take what I want from you now? How would you react? You offer yourself without thought. But what if I do as I please?"

"I don't know," I said, wondering the same thing myself.

He slid his hands in sideways between my legs, grazing my pussy which swelled and ached for more. I was wet almost instantly. He pulled back and then pushed my legs apart with his. I heard his zipper open. I tensed. Was he really going to do this? I had been foolish to fuck with him. He was crazy. I knew that for a fact. Now what? Now I had to wait and see what he was going to do.

Without a word, he pushed his cock, which was quite wide and long, in. I moaned as he began to fuck me. He pulled back, grabbing onto my shoulder to get a better position. Good for him and certainly good for me. I wanted him fucking me like this, dirty and good. That's what it was—dirty and good. Hard and swift. I held onto the sofa and met him thrust for thrust. We fucked so hard, I thought we'd collapse on the floor. Within seconds, we were both coming and coming hard. *It was that good.* He grunted as he came, as his hot semen splashed inside my walls, as he released his lust. My orgasm exploded in my body and made me shake and shiver and once it passed, I fell to the couch, breathing heavily.

He stepped away from me, zipped his pants and left the room, closing the front door softly on his way out. I stared after him, then caught myself in the mirror across the room. I looked like someone who'd just had the fuck of her life. And I was.

I decided to take Sunday off to sleep in. I didn't think he'd mind.

ः

Sven sent me a check the next week. My eyes nearly popped out of my head at the number. I'd never seen so many zeros on a check before. It was sort of like I'd won the lottery, yet on a smaller scale. But no. He wasn't getting off that easily. I sent the check back.

However, he wanted out of this mess and every week thereafter, I'd get a new check from him. Each one was for a little bit more, as if he were tempting me to call the whole thing off, as if he were testing me. I kept sending them back, sometimes with regret. Even though I could have used it, I didn't want his money in this way. I wanted him.

I don't know where I'd turned the corner with him. Before I'd disliked even being around him but suddenly, I wanted him, his cock especially, fucking me. I'd imagine us doing it, almost exploding from all the desire and passion. Suddenly, he looked good and I had to have him. Of course it was the initial spanking that did it. It was that act of control that sparked something in me, that revved up my need and desire and most certainly my lust.

Suddenly, Ted disappeared from my mind. Suddenly, I was no longer worried about the lease on my apartment. The guilt I'd felt over my boyfriend disappeared. Suddenly, all I wanted was Sven. He was all I thought about. It was weird, mainly because I'd only wanted to get away from him before.

On the next Saturday, I arrived at his apartment right at eight in the morning. I let myself in with the key he'd given me and threw my bag on the credenza in the entranceway. I took a minute to look around at the beautiful apartment, so tastefully and expensively decorated, and sighed. Then I took a left and walked into his oversized home office.

His office was designed around several large, floor-to-ceiling mahogany bookshelves that spanned the entire room. In the center of it was a large glass and metal desk that weighed a ton and cost a fortune. He told me once that they had to bring it into the apartment on a crane through the gigantic window. Behind it, his tufted leather office chair. Over to the side was a Chesterfield couch in camel. And looking out the window was Sven.

He was already up and dressed, sipping on coffee—two sugars and a splash, only a splash, of half and half—in a cup that read, "World's Greatest Boss." I knew whoever had given him that cup had been sucking up, obviously. Of course, he might have even given it to himself. He thought he was that wonderful. But in reality, he was the antithesis of a good boss. He was a bad boss. I just wondered why he used this particular cup so much. Did he actually think he was the world's greatest boss? He was that egotistical, so it was a good possibility. However, the irony wasn't lost on me, even if it was on him.

But that didn't matter. When he saw me enter the room ready to work, his eyes widened a little. Without a word, I walked over to his desk, sat down and turned on the computer. Then I turned to him and said, "What's on the agenda today?"

He started to say something but stopped himself. I could tell he was wondering where I was going with this, so he played along. Good choice. He had no idea where I was going but would soon find out. I'd been looking forward to this all week.

"Sven?" I said and adjusted my glasses. "What do we need to get started with today?"

"We need to go over the Larson files," he said, then cleared his throat.

"Let me get them," I said and went over to his filing cabinet.

We worked all day and even through lunch, as usual. He had some sushi delivered and we ate in silence as we worked. Around four in the afternoon, I excused myself to run an errand and returned an hour later.

"What took you so long?" he asked.

I stared at him and wondered why he, of all people, was getting snappy with me. "I dunno," I said. "I had to buy some groceries and things for my apartment. I took the subway. It didn't take that long."

"Chloe, this isn't going to work," he said and got up from his desk and walked over to the couch. He sat down and stared up at me. "It's not going to work."

"Oh, it isn't?" I asked and smiled at him. "What's not going to work Sven?"

"This," he said and waved his hands around as if to illustrate our situation. "Let's stop this. I will hire a new assistant."

Oh, hell no, he wouldn't. *I* was his assistant. There was no way I'd let some new bitch come in here and take my place. He'd fucked me good the other night and he was going to do it again. Sorry, that was just the way it was now. He'd have to understand that.

I knew what made him uncomfortable was the fact that he had lost some control over me. That was fine by me because I liked having some control over him. However, once we started to get it on, then he could take over. He could have all the control he wanted. I wouldn't argue with that.

"Is that what you want, Sven?" I asked and walked over to the desk, taking my place in front of it. "Or is this what you want?"

I began to unbutton my shirt, watching his eyes as I did so. He'd never seen my breasts or felt them before, mainly because when he'd fucked me the other night he'd just gotten down to business and did it without bothering with any foreplay. I could tell he'd been thinking about them, though, as I seductively began to unwrap the gift of my luscious breasts before him. And, yes, they were quite nice. They were a firm C and quite round.

I pulled the shirt open a little and took both hands and lightly rubbed my breasts over my bra. Then I slipped one finger into my bra, touching the nipple as I did so. He couldn't take his eyes off me. I kept rubbing my breasts and watching him, lightly licking my lips as I did so.

"Chloe, this isn't appropriate," he breathed.

"Then how about this? Is this appropriate, Sven?" I asked and turned so that my back was now towards him and my ass was in full view. Then I pulled my panties off, threw them to the side and bent over the desk, spreading my arms out wide, moving his desk accessories and knickknacks out of place. I didn't knock anything off or break anything, but he jumped up from the couch was about to cross over and start straightening things up when I said, "Nuh uh." He stopped and watched me. I began to finger myself, finger my pussy, in front of him. I was so turned on, I almost came. I backed off and turned to him, loving the look of surprise and lust on his face and smiled.

"You know what I want," I said and took off my glasses, throwing them to the side. "Are we on the same page?"

He didn't answer. That was okay. It didn't matter.

I smiled at him and took off my shirt, tossed it to the side then squared my shoulders and walked over to him. I got down on my knees and unzipped his fly and pulled his dick out. It was so hard, it throbbed. I guess my little show did the trick. *Loved* that. I smiled at it, at its thickness. Lightly, I licked the tip of it before sucking it into my mouth. He gasped as I did so, as I gave him a good, hard suck. I continued to do this until I tasted his sweet pre-cum and was about to finish him off when he tugged at my arms, indicating that I should stop. I did so and he bent down in front of me, sliding his hand under my hair and around my neck and pulling my lips to his.

And we kissed. It wasn't a sweet, soft kiss, either. It was hard, with teeth bumping and tongues thrusting and mouths sucking. It was a hungry, *ahhh-give-me-more* kiss. We ate at each other and he pushed me back onto the floor. I fell back and he grabbed at my breasts, squeezing them before unsnapping my bra and pulling it off so they could be free to be sucked and nuzzled and played with. His mouth grabbed onto a nipple and nibbled it, sucked at it and ate at it.

I threw my head back and gasped with the feeling of delight. It felt so good. He kissed my face all over then went to my neck and there he sucked and licked until he went back to my breasts. My chest was red with his pawing at me but I didn't care. I wanted more.

He sat back and ran his hand down my chest to my stomach and to the top of my skirt. He tugged at it until he had it off, so that I was now one-hundred percent naked in front of him. He gave my body a good once over, then pulled my legs apart before bending down and rubbing his nose, just slightly rubbing it, over my pussy until he found my clit.

"Ahhh!" I gasped as the climax hit and as it hit, he grabbed onto my clit with his mouth and sucked at it which strengthened the orgasm.

Once it dissipated, he settled between my legs and stuck his cock in me. I gasped as he immediately hit bottom and then he grabbed onto my head and fucked me. Like that. On the floor. I wrapped my legs around his waist and fucked back, moving my mouth to his so that we could kiss as we enjoyed the feeling of being joined together.

He began to come shortly thereafter, as did I. I squeezed every second of that orgasm out and rode him hard. Once it was over, he fell off me, breathing heavily and staring at the ceiling.

It struck me as odd that he and I had so much pent up passion as most of the time we acted as though we disliked each other. Well, maybe I acted like that. He might have liked me a lot but I couldn't tell as he was one of the oddest people I'd ever been around. But I'd never had sex that good in my life, not even with Ted. I mean, it was good, it was great but this was different. I didn't know why unless fucking someone you slightly loathe makes it more fun. Maybe that was it.

"Chloe," he said. "We must finish our work soon. I have a function to attend."

"Yes, Sven," I said.

He glanced at me and said, "Would you like to accompany me? I don't have a date."

"No," I said and sat up, looking around for my clothes. "I hate those things."

"I will go alone, then," he said. "I won't ask you again."

And he never did.

☙

The next day was Sunday and I, again, took the day off. He didn't call and ask why. He knew why. I suppose it was fine with him. I didn't ask and he never mentioned it.

All week, while I worked at my other job, I imagined us fucking all over his office or in his apartment. I imagined us getting naked in the gigantic shower and letting the warm water spray down on us. I imagined us fucking on the couch in his office. Sometimes I imagined someone walking in on us and finding us doing that, having sex, and wondered what they would think. Would anyone ever imagine that uptight Sven was such a wild man in bed?

I didn't know. I didn't care.

One of the great benefits of us having sex was that he began to really loosen up. He stopped caring so much if everything was perfect. I was pleased but not surprised. Maybe all Sven had needed was a good fucking to make him relax. I know it certainly helped me.

We would always wait until mid-afternoon to start our love making or, as I liked to say, our fuck sessions. I knew he wouldn't relax until he had finished some of his tasks. The wait just made it that much better and built up the anticipation.

And the anticipation was half the fun. I'd start feeling hot the moment I laid eyes on him. My panties would get wet, too, with want. We'd glance at each other every so often and I'd imagine him taking me, throwing me up against the wall and fucking my brains out. A few times I'd smart off to him about something and he'd do that, he'd take me like that. Sometimes he'd just push my skirt up and give me a spanking. That was the best. I *loved* that. I loved being spanked for my naughtiness. The spankings would lead to other things, things like us fucking wildly on his Persian rug or across his desk. It didn't matter how it started as long as it lead to sex.

The more he loosened up, the better the sex got. It got so hot I couldn't stand to be away from him during the week. But I never contacted him to have a quickie or anything like that. And he never contacted me. Even though he was a little more relaxed he was still a slave to his schedule and would not deviate from it. We fucked on Saturday afternoons and that was it. We gave it everything we had until there was nothing left. I had Sunday to recuperate before I went to my real job.

It was odd, but neither of us acknowledged our sex life. We didn't ask questions about boyfriends or girlfriends or any of that. We just took it for granted that this was what we were doing during this time and that was it. It was almost as if we had an ongoing appointment.

"Chloe, I need some milk, please," he said from his desk.

I glanced up at him from my position on the couch. He was really into reading something on the computer.

"Milk," he said. "Please and thank you."

He asked me to do stuff like this from time to time. So, without a word, I went into the super modern and expensive kitchen, got the milk out of refrigerator and poured it into a tall glass. I took it back to him and set it on the coaster beside his hand. As I did so, our hands brushed and we both felt a jolt of electricity. His head jerked up and he stared at me. I stared back and my heart began to pump wildly in my chest.

I went around the desk and sat back down on the couch. He stared at me, then picked up the milk and took a long sip. I took off my glasses, placed them on the side table and turned back to him. He stared at me and without a word, I started to unbutton my white top but he stopped me.

"No," he said, coming around the desk, still holding onto the glass. "Stand."

I almost smiled. It was almost time to get the party started. I stood and he came up beside me and then jerked his head, telling me to get in front of the desk. I did so and waited for his next command.

"Undress," he said.

I had no problem with that. I took my time and unbuttoned my shirt, unsnapped my bra, wiggled out of my pencil skirt and pulled off my panties so I was only wearing my black stilettos. He nodded with approval, surveying my body. It looked good. It was firm and tight and though I wasn't very tall, my limbs were long. Steadying myself with my hands, I leaned back onto the desk and crossed my ankles. If someone entered, they might have expected Sven to have a camera as it looked like we were doing some sort of high-fashion art shoot.

He crossed over to me, still holding the glass of milk and got in real close. I started to tingle as he began to kiss his way down my body, starting with my face, then between my naked breasts and to my flat stomach. Just light, soft and sexy kisses. He came back up and nearly touched my neck with his lips before pulling back slightly and pouring the milk down my shoulder until it streamed down between my breasts. He bent down and began to lap the milk up, licking it off my skin as he did so. It was the most sensual experience I'd ever had in my entire life.

He sucked every drop of milk off my body then turned me around. I went along with him and did as he wanted, bending over the desk and waiting to see what I was going to get.

This time, he simply spread my legs open and pushed his hard cock into me. I gasped and took every long and hard inch he had, even wanted more. Why not? I pushed against the desk and then pushed back against him to get more traction. He pumped into me for a good, long minute then stopped, pulled out and turned me around then put me up on the desk.

My legs opened for him to enter again. But he didn't do that. He took a few minutes to caress my breasts with the backs of his hands, to finger the nipples, to lean forward and give each a light lick and a suck. He did his until I was so pent up with passion I began to finger myself. He stepped back and watched me touching myself. I kept at it, spreading the lips to show him everything, wanting his mouth on it, sucking the juices out.

He stepped back in and pushed my hand away and laid his hand flat against my pussy. I rubbed up against it, feeling his fingers move until they were inside me and the thumb was pressed up against the less explored area of my ass. I moved until he could slip it in and then he finger fucked me. As he moved his fingers around, I ground against his hand, getting so wet I almost slipped off the desk. I was about to come when he stopped, pulled me off the desk and put me up on all fours on the floor.

From there, he slid his hand between my ass cheeks, playing with me, making me moan loudly and start to beg him to fuck me. He kept at it until I was absolutely dripping then he gave his dick a hard stoke and gently, oh so gently, he entered me.

I threw my head back and moaned loudly. Oh, yes. It was so tight and good feeling. It felt so right and so damned dirty I couldn't stand it.

One hand slipped around my body and made its way between my legs and stopped on my clit. As he fucked me, I rode his hand, moving with hard, slow thrusts as he fucked me from behind. It was too much and before I knew it, I was coming, as was he. We both wailed as the intense orgasms hit and shuddered with relief as they passed.

We collapsed on the floor with him on top of me. We lay there for a good few minutes breathing heavily.

After we caught our breath, he stood, held out his hand and helped me from the floor. We walked to the bathroom and he turned on the shower and we got in. He lathered me up from head to toe, taking the washcloth between my breasts and between my legs, giving me a quick, little orgasm before he pushed his mouth onto mine and began to suck at me. I sucked back, throwing my arms around his neck and pulled him into me. He was hard again. He was ready to fuck.

He grabbed me up around the waist and I threw my legs around him, squeezing him into me as his dick found its way in. We fucked slowly, staring into each other eyes, kissing each other's mouth and sucking at each other's necks. We fucked until we came, shuddering with the orgasms and then it was over.

"Chloe," he said. "You are the best assistant I have ever had."

It was the most romantic thing he'd ever said to me. I replied in kind, "I'd never thought I'd say it, but you are the world's greatest boss, Sven."

ℭঃ

"Hey, isn't this that guy you work for on the weekends?" Janie asked and showed me the paper.

I stared at her. She was a co-worker and we were having a quick lunch in the break-room before heading back to work. We'd known each other for years and occasionally went out to dinner at this little Italian place close to my apartment on Sundays. She'd been reading the paper as we talked and ate our deli sandwiches.

"I don't know," I said and glanced over at it, staring at the picture. It was indeed Sven. It was him and another woman, a bimbo, a beautiful buxom blonde, entering into some star-studded charity auction. I had foolishly thought that he attended those things alone after he asked me the first time. Oh, God, what if I'd overplayed my hand? What if I'd acted too aloof? I knew I had him but had I tried to play it too cool? What if I had been too easy? What if he was just using me for sex? What did that mean? Did I want something more? And was he getting something more, via the blonde bimbo? Was she in and was I out? Would she get him to tell her he loved her? He had never said it to me. Would he say it to her? No. He loved no one except maybe, himself.

Fuck. It was over. I knew then and there that it was over. I felt a little panic and wondered what the hell all this meant.

"Chloe?" Janie said and shook the newspaper. "Is that him?"

I didn't let my surprise or shock show and said to her, "Yes, that's him."

"Good looking man," she said. "Now, if you could corral someone like that, you'd have it made in the shade."

She was right. But I hadn't corralled him. After a few minutes had passed and some chitchat, I gave her a smile, excused myself and left the break-room. Then I went into my boss's office and asked her for the afternoon off, telling her I was feeling like I was coming down with something. She obliged and told me she'd see me the next day.

But I wasn't sick. Well, I was. Heartsick. I wanted to go home and cry. That was my intention. When I got there, I grabbed my mail out of my box and took it back to my apartment, threw it on the hall table and started to the couch. But then I noticed something. Sven's check had arrived again today. It was like a sign.

I took the check and sat down on the sofa staring at it. This time it was for a really staggering amount, as if this time he'd really upped the ante to test me. Maybe he wanted me to break it off so he could be free and go back to his OCD ways and his bimbos. Maybe he didn't like me anymore.

I stared around the apartment, remembering that I'd gotten the lease renewal this week. It was time to sign it again for however many years I was comfortable with. No, that's not what I wanted. I was sick of it all, paying for a too-expensive apartment, running the never-ending treadmill that is life in the big city. Trying to get ahead, get ahead, get ahead while keeping up with every other woman in expensive shoes and clothes and purses. It was a rat race and I was losing. I was losing, simply, by running it.

I was over it.

The bottom line was that the check arrived and the lease was up on my apartment. That was where I was. I was there, in that moment. I had what I needed to move forward if I just had the balls to go through with it. It was as if all obstacles were moved out of my way and I was being shown the path to take, the path less taken, the one everyone really wants but is too afraid of undertaking.

I cashed the check.

Without thought, I put all my things into storage and resigned from my job. I bought a one-way ticket to the Cayman Islands and there I finally had the break I had always wanted. And with the money from Sven, I could stay on vacation for a good long while.

၁၃

I rented a small beach house that, while it wasn't directly on the ocean, had spectacular views. I could easily walk to the beach or to the market or wherever. I got a bicycle and would ride around the island on it, letting the soft ocean breeze blow my hair and take my cares away.

But I thought of Sven at least ten times an hour. I thought of what we could have had, if only one of us would have said something. But maybe I'd been right to leave. Maybe I'd been wrong. I just didn't know and that killed me.

I had consigned myself to living a life alone when, one afternoon, the doorbell rang. I had been sitting on the balcony, staring at the magnificent view and wondering how I'd ever *not* been in this place. It was like heaven. It was so serene, so calming, and just so beautiful.

I went to the door, opened it and gasped. It was Sven. As I saw him standing there, I realized how much I'd missed him and how glad I was to see him. I almost threw my arms around his neck and hugged him but something held me off.

"Hello, Sven," I said.

"I have looked everywhere for you," he said. "I was out of my mind with worry."

"Why's that?" I asked, thinking of his blonde bimbo. "What about your blonde bimbo?"

"Huh?" he asked, staring at me. "What blonde bimbo?"

"The one you took to the charity auction."

"She's not a blonde bimbo!" he exclaimed. "That's Melissa, my other assistant. I had to have someone attend with me and no one was available and she said she'd go. Besides, there was a painting there she was interested in bidding on for her husband."

Oh. Fuck. Stupid me. Was I really that stupid? That insecure? Why hadn't I asked? But then I realized why. Maybe I just wanted a change. I had used the blonde bimbo as my excuse. I had wanted to leave, to see if I could live without him. Or maybe, I just wanted to see if he would follow me. And he had. No one knew I was here and yet there he was, not even a week later.

"Chloe?" he said. "Is that why you left? You thought I was cheating on you?"

I shrugged. It was, mostly, the reason why.

"No," he said. "I don't cheat and I would never cheat on you. Never."

I stared up at him and asked, "Why?"

"Because I love you," he said without thought.

I was such a sap, but him saying that meant so much to me. And I loved him, too. I loved his weird OCD thing and I loved his handsome face and I loved the way he'd chuckle when I'd call him on his bullshit. I loved the way we argued and the way we made up. I loved us, together. I loved him. I loved him so much it hurt a little.

But mostly I loved the fact that he had found me, that he had followed me here to this heaven on earth. But I had to say, "What did you say?"

He turned to me and said, "I love you."

His face flushed a little with the words but he didn't let any embarrassment he might have felt back him down from his feelings. He was not a man that said things like that easily so the fact that he'd said it had to be returned in kind. I touched his arm and said, "Good. Because I love you, too."

He smiled at me, gave me a quick kiss to the temple and said, "Why did you come here, Chloe?"

Oh, sure, I could go into a diatribe about feelings or lust or running away. I could talk to him and make him understand where I was coming from, why I had done what I had done. I could explain so many things. But I realized something. I didn't care about anything like that. Living there just that short amount of time had made me take note of life and life was just life. Sometimes you win and sometimes you lose. Today I was winning. Knowing he did love me, that he cared enough to find me, meant so much. Why complicate the feeling with explanation?

I smiled and without a word, took his hand, leading him over to the French doors and walking him through them. I pointed at the crystal blue ocean and the sandy white beach. I said, "This is why I came here and this is why I intend to stay."

He stared at me, then at the scenery, at the striking view. Then he breathed a sigh of relief and said, "I have always, always wanted this. But I have always been too afraid to actually do it. You have shown me many things, Chloe. You have helped me. I am forever grateful."

"I can't go back," I said. "I won't."

He nodded. "That is a good choice."

I grinned at him, loving the fact that he *got* it. Finally! Someone else got it like me. I said, "Sven, are we on the same page here?"

He nodded, smiling at me, showing me with his eyes that he did, in fact, love me. He said, "Yes, Chloe, we are on the same page."

Cold Hard Cash

His name was Cash. Cold Hard Cash. He was hot and he was hard, most all the time. Good for me, I know.

He was the best looking man I'd ever seen. He was the kind of man most women would kill for, with the body to match. He stood tall and proud and dark and handsome, like a Greek god with abs to match. His black hair was cut short so his gray eyes really stood out and they stared with this intensity that was at once hard to define and impossible to look away from.

And he was mine, mine, *mine.* Well, at least until I had to catch a plane back home.

"Go on," he said and waved his hand at the door. "Leave. If you can't handle it, just leave."

But I didn't want to leave, not just yet. If I left, I certainly wouldn't get what I wanted and what I wanted was more sex. He stared at me, looking hurt and a little sad. That was my fault. Well, it was my big mouth's fault. But I couldn't do anything about what I'd said. I'd said I was sorry and I wanted to make amends, if only he'd allow me.

"Go on, Myra," he said. "You need to leave."

I shook my head. Nope, that wasn't going to happen. I mean, you can't give a girl super hot sex one night and then take it away from her the next, can you? That would be downright cruel. It would be bordering on inhumane.

"Please," he said, looking at me. "I don't want to do this."

I watched him closely. He was taking in my body, my face, thinking about all the wild things we'd done last night. He liked what he saw and what he saw was a young woman full of lust for him. Couldn't he see that? Didn't he know how much I wanted him? Did it matter if he did?

He sighed and looked away from me. I didn't like that. I wanted him to look at me, to see me, to see my tight body, my pretty face, and the blue eyes that longed to meet his. He'd told me I was hot, beautiful even. He said he liked my body and my face. He liked me, how I looked, my personality. He'd run his hands through my dark brown hair and pulled it as he made love to me not too long ago.

I wanted him. I knew he wanted me, too. So, I walked over to him, leaning against the wall, and touched his arm before tiptoeing to whisper in his ear, "Do it."

He didn't respond but I could tell he didn't really want me to leave; he didn't really want to "never see you again," like he'd said not even a minute before. There was definitely something between us. It was electric and it made me go against my better judgment. But what did good judgment have to do with this? Nothing much. This was about sex. It was about me and him fucking like crazy and... Not much else.

I slid my hand up his arm and it went to the back of his neck before going into his hair. He narrowed his eyes at me and gave me a look caught between lust and frustration. On one hand, he wanted to do me. On the other hand, he wanted me to pay for being brutally honest with him. He was being cold. He was shutting himself off to protect himself. I could understand that. And I was honest; it was my fault. I'd told him what this was and it was a fling, that's all. Why make it more than that? Couldn't he understand that?

But maybe I was the one who was misunderstanding things. Maybe I couldn't see what he was all about. Maybe it was me and my preconceived notions that had put us in this prickly spot. He was Cold Hard Cash. He thought I only wanted him for his body, to use him. He was like this because of his past experiences, which had nothing to do with me, really. However, that was his line of thinking and his line of thinking was to never let anyone in. If someone got too close, they could judge, they could hurt.

But that wasn't my intention. *Never.* I only wanted to please him and I wanted him to please me. He wanted something more, but was I willing to go the distance? Was he? Could he come out of his shell for one moment and take my hand and maybe lead us in the direction we were meant to go? And where was that? Did it matter? Not now it didn't. What mattered now to me was having him, allowing him to take me. That's what I wanted in that moment. It's all I could see.

I whispered in his ear, "Fuck me, baby, fuck me hard."

He took a deep breath but ignored my request. Fine. I'd get him started. I got down on my knees and tugged at his zipper, wanting to free that big, hard cock. It was in there and it was already ready for me. Why couldn't he just let it do what it wanted? He put too much into this, too much thought, too much worry, too much rumination.

I released his cock from captivity and took it in my hands, rising up on my knees to lick the tip just slightly before putting it into my mouth. That got him going. I knew he wouldn't be able to resist. What man could? In two seconds, he had me lifted up by the arms and thrown against the wall with my back to him. Oh, so this was how it was going to be? A little rough, a little dirty. A little like the way I loved it.

He pushed my legs open and ran his hands up my ass, enjoying its firmness before sliding his hands down my back and into my panties and squeezing it. Ahh, yeah, that felt soooooo fucking good! He bent down and began to eat at my neck as he played with my ass, running his hands up and down sideways before sliding one forward and holding it still on my pussy. Now I could grind, now I could find my groove and get off.

Not so quick. He wasn't going to let me have it that easily. He pushed me against the wall even more and then began to undress me from the waist down. My shorts came off, then my panties. I was half-naked and that felt good. His hand went between my legs, fingering me for a long few seconds before he moved away and bent down behind me. He opened my legs even further so he could stick his head right between them and then his mouth began to work on me, down there.

"Oh, fuck, yes!" I moaned as he began to eat me, devour me, take me with his mouth. Soon, I was grinding against his face, getting everything I could out of it as he sucked at me like I'd just sucked at him. In no time, I was moaning loudly, with passion, and I came with a shudder.

Keeping me against the wall, he kissed his way up my back, then slid his hard cock between my legs. I tiptoed and he stuck it in, all the way in, and then started fucking me, slowly at first until he got some good traction and then with more fervor, harder and harder until I was about to explode once more with orgasm. I placed my hand on my clit and rode it as he rode me, as his mouth sucked at the soft flesh just below my earlobe. It was too much; it felt too good but I couldn't get enough. I was coming and coming so hard I almost fell down. He was close behind, fucking me with everything he had and giving me the best of him. He shot inside of me and then fell onto my back, breathing hard. We stayed like that for a few minutes, until we both caught our breaths.

I turned around, sliding my arms around his neck and kissing him softly, running my tongue across his full lips until he opened his mouth and kissed me back, softly. I moaned, pulled away a little and said, "Aren't you glad I stayed?"

He couldn't help himself. He started to smile, then he cracked up. "Yeah, you could say that."

Thought so.

രു

Oh, so many good things to say about Cash. He was good looking; he was the best lover I'd ever had. He was smart and business-minded. He had a wicked sense of humor and cracked me up almost hourly. He had money. He had style. He had a killer black sports car and a to-die-for condo. There was only one caveat; he was a stripper. A male stripper. Well, I guess that much was obvious. But the thing was he didn't have any of the sleaziness sometimes associated with that job. He, in fact, had a lot to offer, if only I was on board to take it.

However, I was coming off a bad breakup. Actually, it had happened a year earlier but I had a hard time letting go. My ex told me one day that I wasn't *the one.* I had a really hard time getting over that, too. *I* wasn't the *one?* Then why did we stay together almost seven years? I had wasted most of my twenties on him! I thought we were going to get married. I thought we had a future together. I guess I thought wrong.

It also didn't help that my BFF, Becca, had met and married a gorgeous man who lived in San Francisco. And, yes, she moved from our small Georgia town to be with him. She and I had been besties since elementary school and had gone to college together, graduated and then went to work in the same factory as accountants. We saw each other almost every single day. Then one day, she's like, "I'm outta here," and she left. Well, she left after a fabulous wedding and too much cake.

Not long after that my boyfriend broke up with me and I was alone except for my family, of course, and my other friends. But I felt alone most of the time and pretty bad about my situation. Then, out of the blue, Becca called.

"Hey, bitch," she said. "What's up?"

"I'm still pissed off at you," I said.

"What's it this time?"

She sounded so casual. I imagined her sitting in her luxurious apartment twirling her dark brown hair while checking her pretty face reflected in her stainless steel refrigerator. Maybe I was a little jealous but mostly I missed her. I missed our lunches and I missed having her around.

"I'm waiting," she said and sighed.

"You're whooping it up in California and I'm stuck here in peanut land."

She laughed. "Oh, yeah, everyone still grows peanuts there, don't they?"

"They do," I said.

"I've not been here *that* long," she said. "Besides, I'm lonely too. It's hard to acclimate to a big city when you're a small town girl at heart."

I rolled my eyes. "I hate the fact that you're living in one of the most sophisticated cities in the world and still listen to your country music."

"Hey, I love my country music," she said. "Anyway, I have something to cheer you up."

"What's that?"

"I have a trip planned to Miami."

"And how is that supposed to cheer me up?" I asked.

"Because you're invited," she said.

"I am?" I asked. "Who bailed?"

"Brent," she told me. "He has to work. It's sort of like our first anniversary trip but he's covered up at work."

"So, I'm the backup?"

"What's wrong with being the backup if you get to go to Miami?"

I was still feeling sorry for myself, so I said, "I can't do it either. I have a lot of work, too, since one of our accountants quit. Oh, wait a minute, that was you and they still haven't replaced you. Yeah, double work load since you split."

"You're being a baby."

"I'm mad, so I have the right," I said. "And you would not believe the shit they've loaded me down with. I don't get home until after eight every night and then I have to be right back at work by seven. It's getting old."

"So, come to Miami with me."

"I can't."

"You haven't taken a vacation in years," she said. "I know you have the time built up."

"Maybe I plan on using it with someone else."

"Fine," she said. "Be that way. I'll ask Nicki."

"Who's Nicki?"

"My friend," she said. "She lives down the block. We go to the park and walk together. Her fiancé works with Brent."

"You're such a bitch to play that with me," I said. "Like now I'm going to have to jump at the chance to go because I feel insecure that I might be losing my best friend to someone else."

"Exactly," she chimed.

"Fine," I said. "You win. But you're paying for the drinks on the plane."

"I will," she said. "And I'll be happy to."

"Say that after you start paying," I said. "So, am I meeting you in Atlanta and we'll fly down to Miami from there?"

"Yes," she said. "I'm email you the details."

"Okay."

"Well, don't sound so excited."

"I'm excited," I said.

But I wasn't. Not really.

༄

Nicki came with her. I was a little put off at first but the girl was funny and really nice. She was also one of the most stylish women I'd been around and that was because she, herself, was a stylist. She had this great bohemian hippy meets city chic thing going on and it looked great. It went well with her perfect body and blonde hair that looked like she'd been hanging out at the beach to get the perfect color and imperfect wind-swept look. I was totally envious but listened to her suggestions, taking what I had—boyfriend jeans and flip-flops and switching them up with wedges and peasant tops. So, she and I clicked right from the get-go. Becca got food poisoning right when we got there so we left her in the hotel while we prowled the streets, going shopping, barhopping and having a generally fabulous time.

"So, how long has it been for you?" she asked at dinner the second night. "You know, sex. Becca told me you broke up with your boyfriend."

For some reason, I wasn't the least put off by her question. She was the kind of girl, like Becca and I, who talked about sex like most people talk about shoes. It was no big deal to any of us.

"Almost a year," I said and looked out over South Beach. Ahh, it was so nice and we were eating at the yummy restaurant in front of our hotel. It was still hot but there was a nice breeze blowing in from the ocean.

"Wow!" she exclaimed.

"Listen, it's not like I took a vow of chastity or something," I said. "But in my town, inventory is low. If someone is single, there's a reason and it's usually because they're old and kinda crazy or both. And, if they're divorced, they have a ton of kids, which brings complications, to say the least. Otherwise, they're married and gonna stay that way, which is fine by me. Getting married is just something you do."

"But you didn't."

My mouth fell open and she cracked up, squealing with laughter. "Kidding! Kidding! Learn to take a joke, girl!"

"I'm sorry. I don't have a sense of humor," I deadpanned.

She studied me for a second then cracked up again. "You had me!" she laughed, holding the back of her hand over her mouth and looked around, spotting Becca coming towards us. "There's the fuddy-duddy! Quick! Let's pretend we're talking about her!"

Becca flipped her a bird, then fell into an empty chair at the table. "What up bitches?"

"Feeling bad?" I asked and pouted at her.

"Feeling better," she said. "I am never eating a sandwich out of a vending machine again."

"I told you not to do that," Nicki said and took a bite of sushi.

"I was so hungry I had to have something. I don't know what the hell I was thinking," she said and looked me over. "Wow, like the look."

"We went shopping," I sang and grinned then pointed to my dress. "But this is a loaner from Nicki."

"The girl's got a rockin' bod that she totally hides," Nicki said and pointed at me. "But we're working on it."

I almost blushed. Almost. It was good to hear someone appreciated my "bod" because I did run a lot and worked out in the gym when I could. Tonight, Nicki had lent me this killer mini dress that was covered in gold and silver sequins. It fit really loose but showed off my legs, which were lean and now getting quite tanned thanks to the Miami sun.

"She always did," Becca said. "I don't know how she wound up with that loser Trent."

I groaned. "Because he was there, Becca, you know that. And we knew each other and I thought, for some reason, that it was time."

"Time?" Nicki asked and took a sip of sake.

"Time to get married," Becca said. "It's what everybody does in our small town. Besides crazy Alvin Anderson."

"Alvin Anderson?"

"He's a nut, bless his heart," I said. "He walks on the road talking to himself and has crazy hair and dirty clothes... Well, I explained that to you earlier. If they're not married, usually there's a reason."

"And his reason is that he's bat shit crazy," Becca.

"You are so mean!" I said and slapped her arm.

"Oh, I forgot, he almost took you to the prom."

I held up my plate, pretending to smash it against her head. "I am going to brain you over that!"

"What is this about?" Nicki wanted to know.

"She used to work at The Bean, this little diner, and he'd come in there and being the nice person she is, she'd be all nice to him, right? So, during our senior year, he started asking her about prom. She talked to him about it, of course, then asked her to it! When she turned him down, nicely, of course, he threw the cash register through the window."

Nicki's mouth fell to the floor. "Did not!"

"He did," Becca said. "And that's probably why she can't get a date. Everyone thinks her ex is crazy. And he is."

'Shut up!" I screeched. "He was not my ex! He was crazy and, like, twenty years older than me! And I could get a date. I dated my ex for a long time."

"Maybe that's why he wouldn't marry you," Nicki said, laughing.

"Bad girl!" I said and gave her a light punch. "Bad, bad girl!"

She laughed and shook her head at me. "Sorry. I couldn't resist."

Becca gave her a look, then me and said, "No, the reason that asshole wouldn't marry her is because he's a selfish prick."

I groaned. "Becca, let's not go there."

"It's true," she said and crossed her arms. "I told you that you were too good for him. I told you that you were wasting your time."

"Fine," I said. "You were right. I was wrong."

"You got a good friend there, Myra," Nicki told me.

I smiled at Becca. "Yeah, I do."

She smiled back and patted me on the arm. "One day, we will find you a good man. A real man, not some jerkass."

"Could you do it, like, today?" I asked and smiled at her.

"You never know," she said and grinned. "I think you just need to diversify. You'll never find anyone back home."

"Diversify?" I said. "Like you?"

"Like me," she said, very pleased with herself. "I knew there wasn't a man in that town I wanted to marry, so I waited and when my man came into the office looking for the head honcho, I staked my claim."

"So, *that's* how you did it," I said and picked up my iced tea, taking a long sip.

"He was mine," she said. "He just didn't know it yet."

We all cracked up and the waiter came by to ask if we'd like anything else. I asked Becca, "Do you want something?"

"God, no," she said.

"Then just the check please," I told him.

He smiled and handed it to me. I dug into my clutch purse, then handed him my credit card.

"Oh, let me," Nicki said.

"It's on me," I said. "You got lunch."

"Thanks," she said and winked at me. "So, what's on the agenda for tonight?"

Becca shrugged. She still looked like death warmed over. I felt bad for the girl. "Maybe we should stay in tonight," I suggested.

"Oh, no," Becca said. "Don't let me interrupt your good time. You girls go and come back and tell me about all the hot men you see, just like you've been doing since we got here."

"We just like to rub it in your face," I said.

She rolled her eyes at me just as a young man came up on a bicycle and stopped in front of our table. We all stared at him, wondering what he wanted.

"You ladies like dancing?" he asked.

"Who's asking?" Nicki asked.

He shrugged and pulled something out of his backpack, waving it at us. "Free tickets," he said and grinned.

"Free tickets to where?" I asked as Becca grabbed them.

"An all male revue," he said. "It's close by. You can walk, even."

"What the hell is that?" Nicki asked.

"I know what this is!" Becca said and giggled like a teenager. "It's a man meat showcase."

"Man meat?" I asked with a raised eyebrow.

"Male strippers! Duh!" she squealed and waved the tickets in the air. "Hells yeah! We're going!"

"But you're sick," Nicki told her.

"I ain't that damned sick," she said.

"I don't know," I said with uncertainly.

"Come on," she said and held the tickets up. "Wanna go?"

I hesitated for a second too long, giving Nicki the time to grab the tickets and shout, "Yes! We're going!"

So we did.

☙

The young man giving us the tickets informed us that we had to purchase at least one drink each, which was fine by us. Hell, we had two each before the show even started and a third round was on the way.

That's Miami. You come, you play, you get drunk and you do stupid stuff, like go see a man meat showcase, as Becca so eloquently put it.

"I've never been to a male stripper show," I said as I sipped my fruity tropical and very watered down expensive drink.

"Does that mean you've been to a female stripper show?" Becca asked.

Nicki cracked up, shaking her head.

I glared at little at Becca and said, "No, I have not. Have you?"

"Not yet," she said. "But I'm married. Who knows what we'll eventually end up doing to keep things fresh?"

"Oh, God, why did you say that?" Nicki asked. "I'm getting married soon!"

"Just saying," Becca replied and shrugged.

Nicki and I stared at her, then shook our heads, then Nicki turned to me and asked, "So, you've never been to an all male stripper show before?"

"I have not," I replied.

"I've been to a few bachelorette parties," she said, glancing around the room from our table in the back. "Wow. There are a lot of bitches in here."

There were. I mean, a *lot*. This must have be a popular revue because every woman in Miami, and probably the surrounding county, had showed for it. The room was gigantic, too, almost like a small theater or something.

"What are they called again?" Becca asked.

I shrugged, noting that the thought of seeing male strippers had miraculously healed her and she was looking better. She'd gone up to our room to change into a nice striped top and a pair of skinny jeans with heels, almost the exact same outfit that Nicki had on. Suddenly, I wanted my jeans too and not this expensive and very beautiful mini dress that Nicki had let me borrow. What if I spilled a drink on it? Nicki would probably kill me.

"They're called Hard Working Men," a nice looking lady at the next table told us as she adjusted her straight-out-of-the-eighties high hair.

Her friend in the next seat chimed in, "Yeah, they're the Men of Construction, that's the name of this revue. It's about construction work."

"Yeah, I get that," Becca said a little smart-assed. "Men of Construction. Hard Working Men."

"No," the other one sassed. "They are the Hard Working Men, that's the group name and this showcase is called Men of Construction. They do different kinds of shows with different themes, you know."

We just stared at her, wondering why she was acting so much like a fangirl. I didn't get it. But I soon would.

"Thanks for the tip," Becca said sarcastically and picked up her drink, laughing a little to herself.

"No problem," the woman said and nodded eagerly. "You'll want to come tomorrow, too. We try to come down and see them at least a couple times a month."

"Nice," I said and glanced at Becca who surmised her with a raised eyebrow. She stared at me and we hid our smiles. I knew then and there that she was still my best friend and would always be. It was nice to know. I stared at her and exclaimed, "I've missed you so much!"

"I've missed you too!" she said and hugged my neck, almost drunkenly. "Myra, you have to move to San Francisco with me! I need my best friend!"

"Hey! What about me?" Nicki asked.

"I'm not forgetting about you. All three of us would be so cool together," she said and stared at me. "We could open a cupcake shop!"

"Now you're getting crazy," I said. "And drunk," I added and shook my head, taking the drink out of her hand. "You have nothing on your stomach, so stop."

"Whatever, Mom," she said sarcastically.

"I've known you since second grade," I told her. "I know how you are. If you drink too much, you'll be passed out in less than an hour."

"Fine," she said and waved at a passing waiter. "A water, please."

He nodded and walked past us.

"When the fuck is this going to start?" Nicki whined.

"Eight-forty-five," our friend at the other table said. "We've still got five minutes."

"Five minutes?" Nicki asked. "Think I have time to run to the ladies room?"

"No way," the woman said. "What if they start early? You could miss the opening."

"That's true," Nicki said.

The waiter came back with the water. I took it, unscrewed the cap and handed it to Becca. "Drink."

"Fine," she said and took a long sip. "But seriously, get the show on the road, fellas! I want to go to bed and call my honey."

"You miss your hubby?" Nicki asked.

"No, I miss my bed," she said and pouted. "I just got this divine mattress. It's this—"

She was interrupted when a loud noise that sounded like a jackhammer ripped into the room. Then the lights went out, leaving us in total darkness.

"It's starting!" Becca giggled. "It's starting!"

"Shh!" the ladies at the next table hissed.

She sat back and shut her mouth. I stared at her and we almost started laughing but I shook my head and turned my attention to the darkened stage.

"Ladies and gentlemen…" the emcee started, then cleared his throat. "I mean, ladies and ladies please welcome Hard Working Men!"

He said it like this: Hard! Working! Men!

And welcomed they were. Every woman in the house was up and out of her seat, shaking ass and screaming as a group of good looking, muscular and, apparently, hard working men came onto the stage. Wow. I mean, WOW! Okay, I'd give it to them. They were a bunch of hard working men who were also man meat. Becca had been right in her description of them. They were also the Men of Construction. And, damn, they looked good.

The show started. I thought for a second that *Y.M.C.A.* would start playing but instead, I heard the undeniable sounds of *Shake Your Money Maker*—the Black Crows version—start playing. And that's what got my ass out of my seat. It was, like, one of my all-time favorite songs. Ever. Again—ev-ah!

The first Man of Construction came to the front of the stage with a shovel. He was shirtless and dressed in a pair of blue jeans, work boots and yellow hard hat which, apparently, was the costume for all of the men—and he started dancing with it like it was a very tiny woman. I thought it would be hokey but it was actually very well choreographed and worked. He dipped her, touched her head and then her body as the crowd went absolutely bat shit crazy.

And we went crazy with them. Nicki, Becca and I were out of our seats, almost ready to climb up and dance on the table as the music pounded in our ears and the men onstage revved us up.

The next guy came out with a jackhammer and, literally, started jack-hammering. The thing shook him or he shook it—I wasn't sure which. Nicki leaned over and yelled in my ear, "How'd you like to get jack-hammered by him!"

I laughed so hard I doubled over. But, yeah, that wouldn't have been a bad thing. Sure, why not? But then I really thought about it. That *would* be nice. I noticed how all the women in the room were acting and they were acting like they wanted that, they wanted to be jack-hammered by this guy or one of his coworkers. The energy was palpable and it kept building and building. I didn't know what it was or what had happened, but since the show had started there seemed to be this personality change occurring. Every woman in there, ourselves included, was acting different. We were acting wild and totally uninhabited. I'd never danced or laughed or, well, felt this hot in my life. And by hot, I mean, sexy. I felt so sexy and alive, I was almost beside myself.

And the men on the stage were the reason why. They were beyond hot. Sure, it might have been a little sleazy, but who cared? It was fun! It was sexy and it was something I needed. I couldn't take my eyes off the stage and I never wanted the show to end.

The next Man of Construction came out with a measuring tape, whipped it out and laid it against his leg, nodding knowingly at the crowd. We laughed so hard we had tears streaming down our cheeks. This really was the most fun I'd had in... Well, ever.

I picked up my drink and took a sip.

"I'll give them this!" Becca yelled. "Those guys sure know how to use their tools!"

I did a spit-take. Nicki and Becca collapsed in laughter as soon as I did it then I started laughing too, then yelled at them to stop as we were missing the show. We turned out attention back to the stage where yet another Man of

Construction came out with a, yes, nail gun. A nail gun! For some reason, I'd always wanted one of those things. I used to tell my ex I was going to get one for when I did projects around my house. And he told me I'd shoot myself in the hand and have to go the emergency room.

He was always such a killjoy. I was suddenly glad I was free of him. I smiled to myself, realizing I was over him, I was over my ex! And all it took was a few good looking strippers. Had I known this, I would have been going to all male revues all along.

The nail gun guy pretended to accidently shoot everyone on stage and they fell like flies, then he acted like there was something wrong with the nail gun and started looking at it. Then he pretended to accidently shoot himself and fell down. The stage went dark and a spotlight came on in the middle then fog began to pump in the spotlight and swirl around and then the music died down.

The crowd went quiet for a long for seconds. What was going on? I had to see. I kicked off my heels and with the help of Becca and Nicki, climbed up onto the table. And there I saw him for the very first time. He came out without any apparatus but he did have a yellow hard hat on as well and was carrying a set of blueprints. While his chest was bare, he wore a pair of khakis with his work boots.

I couldn't believe how quiet the room got. I looked around, wondering why, then turned my attention back at the stage at the latest man. He stood in the middle of the stage with his head down as if he were waiting for his cue. And then he got it.

"Cold! Hard! Cash!" the crowd roared. "Cold! Hard! Cash! Cold-Hard-Cash! Cold Hard Cash! Cold Hard Cash!"

"What are they saying?" Nicki asked Becca, who shrugged.

I was about to tell her but I couldn't take my eyes off of him, this Greek god before my very eyes. His muscles... Oh, his muscles, ripped to perfection and just so delectable. I'd never in my life seen such a man. He had no fat on him whatsoever. But he didn't look like he'd taken drugs to get that body, either. It looked very natural and strong and just… Yummy.

He looked up just then, glancing at the crowd from beneath his yellow hard hat. And then he and I locked eyes. I mean, I think we did. Yeah, we did. But it was probably just my imagination. Just like everybody else there, I wanted to be the girl in the crowd that he liked best.

"Cold! Hard! Cash!"

I didn't get why they were chanting this, but it was okay by me. But did it mean that I was supposed to start throwing money at him? I didn't know Cash was his name or that he was *the* male stripper every woman who loved male strippers knew about and went crazy for. I didn't know anything about him, of course, but there he was and I knew there was something about him I liked. I mean, I liked the other guys, too, but he was different.

The Nazareth song *Hair of the Dog* started playing. Swear to God! I hadn't heard that song in years.

"What are they saying?!" Becca asked our friend at the next table.

"That's Cold Hard Cash, lady!" she screeched, saying it like she was ready to throw down. "He's the man!"

"Show some respect!" her cohort snipped. "He's playing the supervisor! Cold Hard Cash! He's the boss!"

Oh, that was his name, his stage name—Cold Hard Cash. That was cool. I kinda liked it.

"Whatever," Becca said and turned her eyes back to the stage.

Cold Hard Cash stepped forward and then turned around. As soon as he did that, all the other men jumped up and got into position and then the show started. The Men of Construction were now doing what they did best and that was giving the ladies a show. They began to dance to the music and then, all at once, they leaned down and pulled their pants off in one fell swoop. I'd never seen such a creative use of Velcro before. Now they were standing there showing everyone their quite stylish black boxer briefs, which were very short. But that wasn't what everyone was paying attention to. They were all staring at what the men were packing and what they were packing was jaw-dropping good. Every eye in the crowd was on the enormous bulges that were being prominently, and quite proudly, displayed. I couldn't take my eyes off them, either. They were so big!

"Thank God they don't have banana hammocks!" Nicki yelled, laughing.

I laughed and kept my eyes on the stage, fascinated that not only were they good dancers but they were actually dancing to a Nazareth song, which, in and of itself, was quite a feat. Cold Hard Cash walked across the stage and jerked his head at each of the other men as if he were giving them their lunch breaks. One by one, they stepped off the stage and into the crowd of waiting women. If I were them, I might have been a little scared as the women were almost at a fever pitch. They were getting hot and horny. But how could they not? Those bulges were something else! I mean, were they real? Were all the Men of Construction packing? If so, I wanted to see more and by more I mean, I wanted them to drop trou.

Yeah, I did.

There were plenty of men to go around, but still there was a shortage. Women were vying for their attention, waving dollar bills in the air and yelling at them to come to their tables. Each guy had about ten or so women all over him as they stopped and gave quick lap dances and pecks on the cheek. The women were beside themselves and started pushing dollar bills into their undies. It was insane! I saw women grabbing asses and pushing out their chests and wiggling their boobs at the men. One woman literally took one of the men's hands and placed it on her boob, making him squeeze it. I'd never seen anything like it before in my life.

"Somebody's horny!" Becca laughed.

I nodded. That was true, me included. There was so much sexual aggression—on the women's part—it was almost surreal.

But it was so fun. Nicki, Becca and I laughed at what we were seeing and danced like crazy. I stopped for a moment to look up and locked eyes with Cold Hard Cash. Wow. And then... Then I noticed something unusual. Cold Hard Cash was headed my way!

No way. But maybe he wanted to speak to the ladies at the next table. They certainly seemed to be hardcore fans. But no. He came to our table—I was back in my seat by then—and grabbed my hand, pulling me close to him and started dancing very dirty which was fine by me. He felt good being so close to me and he started nuzzling my hair, then running his head up and down my body. I was almost beside myself and slightly embarrassed. But then again, how are you supposed to feel in this type of situation? I didn't know so I held on for the ride. And the ride entailed him putting his big hands on my body and even on my ass. Was he even supposed to be doing this? Was it legal? I didn't know and I really didn't care. It felt *good.* I swear, I could have thrown him down on that table and climbed on top of him. I wanted to. I don't know why I had this change occur, but it was like this new person had taken over. But then I realized it was the atmosphere; the Hard Working Men were doing just that—working each and every one of us, almost to a froth. I knew there were plenty of husbands and boyfriends gonna get laid tonight. I just wished I had someone whose bones I could jump.

Then he was done with me. He continued to hold onto me, placing his hand on the small of my back. My face was so hot I knew it showed, even in the darkened room. Becca and Nicki watched and laughed their asses off at us.

"You're the most beautiful woman in here," he whispered in my ear.

"I bet you say that to all the girls," I said loudly.

"No," he replied. "I don't."

I blushed again and said, "Well, you should."

He grinned and said, "Touché."

Then he twirled me around and set his sights on Nicki. They danced but I noticed he didn't put the moves on her that he had on me and that made me feel really, really good. Maybe he did like me. Just a little. Another Hard Working Man then showed up and took Becca's hand and they danced. And, yet another Hard Working Man showed up and he got behind me, shoving himself right up on me in a very aggressive way. Cold Hard Cash gave him a look and he moved away from me and on to our friends at the next table who seemed more than pleased that he'd decided to give them his attention.

I didn't know what to do next so I grabbed my drink, then glanced at Cold Hard Cash who was walking back over towards me. Without a second thought, I grabbed a twenty out of my clutch and held it up, waving it at him and grinning like a fool. He grinned back, came over to me, took the twenty and then shoved it down into my bra. I nearly fell over. Becca and Nicki woohooed, shaking their fists in the air.

"Why'd you do that?" I asked.

"Because I ought to be tipping you," he said and then gave me a quick kiss on the cheek before turning and disappearing into the waiting and wanting crowd.

I turned to Becca and Nicki who grinned at me and yelled, "Woohooo!"

Yeah, woohooo!

But the show wasn't over yet. The Hard Working Men were now making their way back to the stage. We watched with rapt attention as they got on, turned their backs to us and then, with one quick tug, pulled off their black undies. A line of bare asses stared at the crowd. The women went ballistic and started chanting, "Turn around! Turn around! Turn around!"

We got into it, each of us joining in and chanting, "Turn around! Turn around! Turn around!"

And then they did! And each of them had an enormous dong with just a little white sock covering it from the world.

"Holy fucking shit!" Nicki yelled. "I can't believe they pulled a full monty!"

"They didn't!" Becca yelled over the crowd. "That's a banana hammock!"

"No!" I corrected. "That was a sock!"

And, boy, wouldn't I have loved to see what that sock was hiding. Booyah!

ಜ

Naturally after that, we did what all self-respecting women would do after seeing an all male revue and went out for drinks. There are a lot of bars in South Beach, so we found a nice place right away and ordered some martinis. After we were almost loaded to the point we couldn't walk, Becca got her appetite back and forced us to find somewhere to eat. Luckily, there was a diner close to our hotel and we walked there, laughing about the show, telling each other we were coming back soon.

At the diner, we practically dove into our bacon, eggs and big stacks of pancakes. Ah, I was either so drunk I didn't care or the food was so delicious that it just melted in my mouth. I don't think any of us said a thing until about half the food was gone.

"Well, the Men of Construction certainly know how to please women," Nicki said finally and dabbed her mouth with a napkin. "They're good looking and ready to do some work around the house, if you know what I mean."

"Yeah, all women love to see a man working," Becca said and grinned.

"Especially in the bedroom," I said with a raised brow.

"Oh, my God, you're worse than those women who were sitting next to us," Nicki said. "Girl, you gotta get laid."

"And soon," I agreed.

"Like tonight, right?" Becca said and pointed at my plate. "You gonna eat that last piece of bacon?"

"Have at it," I said and pushed the plate way. "There goes my diet."

"Like you need to diet," Nicki scoffed.

I shrugged and asked, "What time is it?"

"Almost two in the a.m.," Becca said and looked around me towards the cash register, then her mouth dropped open. She said excitedly, "Oh, my God, is that Cold Hard Cash?"

I looked over my shoulder to get a look. I couldn't believe it. Becca was right. It really was him. He was speaking to the night manager from across the counter. I noticed that he was dressed casually, almost like a surfer, in a slightly too big for him t-shirt, cut-off khakis and beat-up leather flip-flops. He looked very cool, even with his clothes on. Then he glanced our way, did a double-take and broke out into a big grin. I couldn't help but grin back.

Then, out of nowhere, Becca and Nicki started chanting, "Cold! Hard! Cash! Cold! Hard! Cash!"

"Shh!" I hissed.

"Cold! Hard! Cash!" they chanted, grinning at me.

He shook his head, smiling, and headed our way. I ducked down a little, slightly embarrassed. I mean, he was probably the best looking guy I'd ever seen and he'd kissed me on the cheek and even groped me a little. Of course, he'd probably kissed—and groped—a lot of women, so I maybe I shouldn't have felt that special.

"Hello, ladies," he said with a slight Southern drawl.

"Hello, Cash," Nicki said and smiled at him. "Is that your real name?"

He shook his head, laughing a little. "It is. The cold and hard came later, after I started, you know… Dancing."

"I like it," she said and gave him a wink.

He grinned and glanced over at me, then back at her, then said, "Well, thank you."

"Is that a Southern accent I detect?" Becca asked. "Not from Miami?"

"Actually, I from farther south," he said and glanced at me again, then back at her. "South Carolina."

We cracked up at his joke, laughing like little school girls. He was so funny. And cute. And hot. And sexy. And… Oh, good God, thank you for allowing us mere mortals to be in the presence of such a man. They do exist!

"Oh, South Carolina," Becca said. "Whereabouts?"

"A little town just outside of Myrtle Beach," he said.

"Myra and I took a few spring breaks there a few times, didn't we, girl?" Becca said and smiled at him.

"We did," I said and nodded.

"Oh?" he said. "Is that so?"

I nodded. "Yup. Couldn't get too far from Georgia."

"What part of Georgia?" he asked.

"Middle," I said and refused to look him in the eye. Actually, I couldn't even look at him. He was so cute, it made me nervous. Even though I was sure I was blushing, I didn't want him to know I liked him. What sort of fool would I look like? I glanced down at my gigantic plate of food and pushed it away and said hurriedly, "I usually never eat this much."

Nicki and Becca raised an eyebrow each at me.

He chuckled and said, "Don't worry about it. It's good food." He paused. "I'll tell you what will make it even better. It's on me." He motioned to the manager who nodded, then turned back to us. "Have a lovely evening, ladies," he said and smiled as he turned to walk away.

"It's Nicki, Becca and Myra!" Nicki said and pointed at each of us.

He backed away laughing and nodded, then exited.

"He has to be the coolest guy in the world," she said. "Is he not? Is he not the coolest guy in the world?"

"He is! He is!" Becca and I chimed in.

"Oh, how I wish I wasn't engaged," Nicki said.

"How I wish wasn't married," Becca said, then stared at me. "You know what, Myra? You should go for it. He's cute and I could tell he digs you."

"Are you serious?" I asked. "And how am I supposed to 'go for it?' Just walk up to him and ask him to sleep with me?"

"That'd work," Nicki said. "I would."

Becca nodded. "Me too."

I shook my head. Yeah, I wanted to get laid but I didn't want to act desperate. Was I desperate? I thought about it. I probably was. But not *that* desperate.

"He's a stripper," Nicki said. "Women do it to them all the time. It's not like he's never been approached like that before."

"I don't think I want to," I said. "Sorry, but I just don't. He's cool and cute and all but... You know, I still have a little pride and I don't like to beg."

"If I were single," Becca said. "I'd beg. For him, I'd beg."

"Well, I'm not going to," I said. "Come on. Let's go."

They shrugged and we left a tip on the table and left. Then Becca wanted to walk on the beach. We went across the street and walked in the surf, almost getting soaked from head to toe. Then we sat down on the sand near the water and fell back laughing. The waves gently lapped at our feet.

"We're like a bunch of teenage girls," Nicki said. "What did they put in our drinks?"

"Fun," Becca said and propped herself up on her elbows then grimaced. "Oh, fuck! My stomach! I shouldn't have eaten!"

"Oh, shit, you okay?" I asked and sat up.

"I'm fine," she said. "I just need to lie down. You two stay here and I'll see you back at the room."

"You sure?" I asked.

She nodded and smiled, then grimaced. "I'm never eating again!" she yelled as she ran off.

"Poor thing," I said and stared after her. "Maybe I should go see about her."

"No, you stay," Nicki said. "I'll see if she's okay. Unless, of course, you want to come too?"

I stared out over the waves and felt so peaceful, I shook my head. "No, if you don't mind, go on. I'll be up in a little bit. If you need me, I have my cell."

"Will do," Nicki said and followed Becca back to the hotel.

I sighed and lay back in the sand, loving the fact that I was here, in Miami. Was there any better place to be? I didn't know but for a second I wanted to sell everything I had and move down here. It was just so addicting. But then I realized that I'd be alone as Becca and Nicki were going back to San Fran and I had no relatives or friends here. I wasn't so sure how much fun it would be when it was just me by myself.

"Nice out, isn't it?"

I looked up to see Cold Hard Cash. I was so immersed in my thoughts I hadn't noticed him standing there. He was barefoot and looking so cute and sexy it hurt a little. I had a hard time coming up with anything to say but finally managed to mumble, "Yeah, it is nice."

"I walk on the beach every night," he said. "I'm sort of an insomniac after a show. The adrenalin gets going and it takes a while to calm down."

I nodded and sat up, brushing the sand off of me. "So, that was a good one, that show," I said and shook my head. What was I saying? Was I still mumbling? Was I coherent? I didn't know but he smiled and sat down beside me.

"Thanks," he said. "We try. You girls here on a bachelorette party trip?"

"Huh? Us? Oh, no. Well, Nicki, the blonde, is engaged but Becca is already married and me... Well, I'm single." There I went again. Like I was telling him so he'd know I was available. Dufus! What the hell was wrong with me?

"Cool," he said. "I just thought that maybe you three were here because of that. We get a lot of bachelorette parties."

"Never cared for them that much myself," I said. "We threw Becca a shower, but that was it. She was ready to get the hell out of town and couldn't be bothered."

"Oh?" he asked.

I nodded. "She lives in San Francisco now. So does Nicki. I'm the only one still on the East Coast."

"It's the best, though," he said.

I laughed a little. "It is. I agree."

"Cool," he said. "You like Miami?"

"I do," I said. "How did you get down here? From South Carolina, I mean?"

"I drove," he said.

I stared at him and then we cracked up. "No, I mean, how... Never mind. I shouldn't pry."

"No, pry all you like," he said. "I came down here to model—shocker, I know. And then that sort of petered out and I needed money and there was a show that hired me. And then, well, the rest is, as they say, history."

"Cool," I said and smiled at him. "By the way, it's cool that you're cool. I mean, you're cool, not weird. Does that make sense? I mean, you're, like, a normal guy. You're cool. Cool." I shook myself. How many times could I say "cool" in a sentence? Why didn't I try to slip a few more in there? Argh! I was such an idiot.

"We all are, normal and cool," he said. "This is just how we make our living."

"I know," I said, noticing how all of a sudden the alcohol really started kicking in. I was a little bit drunk, to say the least. "Just excuse me. I've had one too many martinis tonight. Not to mention fruity tropical drinks."

He nodded and looked out over the waves and was about to say something when all of a sudden a huge wave came up to the shore and soaked us from head to toe.

"Oh, fuck!" I said and felt the sting of salt water in my eyes.

"I was about to say we were too close to the water," he said and jumped up and then held out his hand to help me up.

I got up then stared down at the dress and shook my head. "Nicki is gonna be pissed."

"You borrow that?" he asked.

I nodded. "Unfortunately. Now I am up shit creek."

"It still might be okay," he said and held up the shoulder to get another look, then dropped it. "No, that dress is fucked."

The dress was completely soaked and weighing me down. I wanted out of it as it felt kind of icky now. Sea water and sequins, they do not go together.

"Shit! I knew it!" I said. Then, for some reason—maybe it was all the liquor, maybe it was because I had on this super heavy dress that was now soaked with ocean water and smelled a little fishy—I sort of forgot he was there or didn't give a shit and pulled the dress over my head and threw it on the sand. I glanced down at my body, noticing my panties and bra were soaked, too, and very uncomfortable. I glanced up at him, standing there, staring at me, and I suddenly felt so free. Free to do whatever I wanted to do. I grinned at him and unhooked my bra. Besides, I was pretty drunk so I didn't really care what anybody thought at that moment.

"Don't do that!" he yelled and held his hand up.

"You do it for a living!" I said. "I'm doing it now!"

"What is wrong with you?" he asked.

Nothing was wrong! Everything was fine! Sure, I wasn't acting like myself but what was the big deal? I never got to act crazy and do stuff like this. I did everything by the book and I was sick of it. For tonight, I wanted to be that free person I knew was inside of me. I wanted her to come out and play. While I was feeling tipsy, the fact of the matter was that I wasn't too drunk not to know what I was doing, but drunk enough not to care. Besides, I knew I probably wouldn't be coming back here for a long time. So, why not? I wanted to see how far I could take this. Life was short and I needed to get some living in. This was my moment.

I threw my bra at him and held my arm over my breasts, grinning. I turned to the ocean which seemed to welcome me. Fuck it! I was going for it! I ran into the water, almost tripping in the waves and dove in. Salt water stung my eyes but I didn't care. I was free! I'd never felt so free! I probably should have watched my alcoholic intake but oh, well! I turned to see Cold Hard Cash coming towards me, as if he were going to rescue me and I yelped, dove in and tried to swim away. But he grabbed me by the foot and pulled me to him. He forced me on my feet and grabbed onto my shoulders.

"You're drunk," he yelled over the surf. "You could drown! Come on!"

"I am not drunk!" I said, realizing that I was turned on from the show and definitely from him. "I'm happy!"

"Good for you!" he yelled. "Come on!"

And, in a fit of either temporary insanity, which I'd already aptly displayed, or in a fit of lust, which had been building since I laid eyes on him, I threw my arms around his neck and kissed him. And I mean *kissed.* I half-expected him not to kiss back and he didn't at first, as if me kissing him shocked him but then he did and he kissed back as if he were pleased I'd kissed him first. Sometimes a girl can make the first move. Especially in this case.

"Oh God," I moaned, allowing the atmosphere and the lust in my body to take over. "Fuck me, Cold Hard Cash," I moaned. "Fuck me."

"You're drunk," he said, still kissing me.

Yeah, drunk with lust. "Come on," I said and ran my lips over his again. "Let's do it."

"Are you sure?" he asked and pressed his body closer to mine.

"I am," I moaned wanting it so badly I couldn't think straight. And it had been a while for me. I needed sex and he was there. Why the fuck not?

He stared at me and nodded. "If that's what you want."

I didn't answer. I pushed myself onto him and kissed him again, kissed him hard, ramming my tongue into his open and waiting mouth, allowing him to suck at it then offer me his to suck on and to play with. We ate at each other and my nipples rose up in need, needing to be toyed with, needing to be touched and suckled and pinched, just a little. And then he did. His big hands came up and cupped my bare breasts, squeezing them and then he pinched the nipples, a little harder than I expected but that just added to the intensity of the situation. And the situation was that we were standing in the ocean. I was nearly naked and he was kissing me, playing with my nipples and I wanted more.

"Touch me down there," I whispered in his ear and nibbled at his earlobe. "Between my legs. Touch me. Please, touch me."

He complied and cupped me there, down there, squeezing me gently as his mouth found mine again and began to suck at my lips. He bent me back a little so that my hair was in the water, then pulled me back up. I jumped into his arms, wrapping my legs around his waist and he walked us back to the beach and laid me down on the sand.

My hands were in his short hair, grabbing at it, pulling at it, then they went down his back, along his strong back. He rose up and pulled his soaking shirt off and threw it to the side. I grabbed onto his pants, slipping my hand inside them and found his cock. Oh, wow. He was hung. He was big and I mean *big*. I'd never felt one quite that large but it pleased me to no end. Sure, I had gotten an idea of how big it was at the show, but to see and touch it in real life was quite another thing entirely.

I pulled at his shorts until they came off him along with his boxers and then he was naked. But I still had my panties on. He kissed my lips, then my cheek, sliding his tongue along my neck and then between my breasts and down my stomach. He paused at the top of my panties then grabbed hold of them with his teeth and pulled them off until I was naked like him. He began to eat at me a little, moving my legs apart until I moaned. I let him go for a good few minutes but then I knew what I wanted and what I wanted was his hard dick inside of me.

I tugged at his shoulders until he kissed his way back to my mouth and my legs opened wide. He settled between them and then he was in. Ahh! Fuck! Yes! His dick felt so good, like it needed to be there, inside of me, fucking me. And fuck me he did. It didn't take me a minute to get my groove on before I was pushing against him, grabbing onto his ass and getting as much out of him as I could get before the orgasm hit. And when it hit, it hit hard. I let out a wail as it came at me and claimed me as its own.

He was right there with me and he finished right after me. We kissed as the orgasms swept through our bodies and kept kissing until they left us panting and wanting more. He stayed on top of me, inside of me, owning me for a long moment before he fell off and breathed heavily, staring up at the sky.

"Wow," I said and propped my head up with my elbow. "That was fan-fucking-tastic!"

He grinned. "It was, wasn't it?"

I kissed him, licking his lips as I did so, then pulled back. "I never did anything like that before."

"Me either."

I leaned back and stared at him. "What?"

He eyed me. "What do you mean *what?*"

"I mean, what," I said. "You've never had sex on the beach before. *You?*"

"No," he said, then paused. "Does that come as a surprise?"

"Well, yeah, you're a stripper," I said.

"It doesn't make me a man whore," he said.

"Oh," I said and thought about it. "So, I'm your first, sort of like you're a virgin?"

He cracked up. "In a way, yes."

"Cool," I said and bit my bottom lip. "Just so you know, I'm not a slut. I don't do stuff with every guy I meet. And it's been a while for me and I was a little drunk and—"

"Shh," he said and pulled me to him, kissing me softly. He pulled back and stared me dead in the eye. "No need to explain."

I smiled and then I stared at him, at his handsome face and those eyes... I couldn't get over how gorgeous they were, those eyes, how beautiful and gray with the thick black eyelashes. I could get lost in them, like in some country song or something. I began to feel something then, something I'd never felt before. It was totally new and it felt right. I didn't know it, but I was sure I was feeling love, real love, genuine love. And the way he stared back at me, I knew he felt it too.

I wanted him again. I wanted him so badly. I leaned over and whispered in his ear, "Take me home and fuck me again. I'll let you do whatever you want to me as long as you fuck me."

I'd never said anything like that to a man before but I was beside myself with lust. I had to have him again. Now.

He moaned as I kissed at his lips, then pushed me back gently. "Okay, but first you need to put your dress back on."

"Maybe you should put your clothes back on, too," I said.

So he did and I did. We put our still wet clothes on and then we walked to his condo which was just two blocks from the beach. I didn't get a good look at it. I think it was nice, but I didn't really care what it looked like. I just wanted to know where the bed was.

We didn't have time to find it because we were kissing and coming out of our wet clothes as soon as he opened the front door. He pressed his naked body against mine, kissing me deeply. He was hard and ready. I was wet and ready. It was time.

He bent me over the arm of his couch and pushed my legs open. And then he eased it in, his hard cock filling me up. He leaned over to squeeze my breast with one hand before he started fucking me. Soon, he was power-driving into me. I couldn't do anything but hang on for the ride and what a ride it was.

"Ahh!" I moaned, loving every second of it. "Ahh! Yes!"

Then he gave my ass a good, hard slap. "Ouch!" I exclaimed, a little surprised. But then he rubbed it a little and I realized I liked it and wanted another. He gave it to me, slapping my ass hard before squeezing it.

"Oh, yeah," I said and rose up, grabbing his hand and bringing it to my breast so he could squeeze it. He licked at my neck and fucked me from behind and it was almost too much to take. I bent back down and he fucked me some more. It was good and dirty and like nothing I'd ever experienced. I wanted more.

I pushed against him then he stopped and pulled out, turned me over onto my back and pushed me back onto the couch. He settled between my legs and his cock slipped right in, like it belonged there. And we slowed down, almost methodically, and we fucked. He kissed me as he fucked me, sucked at my neck and then bent to take a nipple into his mouth. I arched away from the couch at that and then I felt it. I felt the orgasm. It was quick and it wanted release. Before I could stop it, it came at me and I grabbed onto him, digging my nails into his back as I came and came hard.

He pumped into me and then pulled out and squirted his hot cum all over my stomach. I rubbed it into my skin, staring him in the eye as I did so, then tasted it from my fingers. His mouth dropped as I did that and I grinned at him, loving just how dirty I was getting. But then again, it was his fault. He had brought it out in me.

"Wanna stay over?" he asked.

"I thought you'd never ask," I replied.

⚃

Yeah, his condo was cool. After we took a long shower together to get the smell of the sea off each other, we plopped into his big bed. The sheets were of a very high thread count and felt divine on my naked skin. Then we went to sleep. Yeah. For the first time in my life, I slept naked. I was doing a lot of firsts—going to an all male revue, meeting a handsome stripper on the beach, having wild sex. Miami was turning out to be the best time ever.

I awoke with the sun streaming in from the French doors that lead out onto the balcony. Cash was nowhere around. I smiled to myself, thinking of all the downright naughty things we'd done last night and snuggled into the bed. Then I looked around at all the tasteful furnishings. The bed had this cool weathered leather headboard and the nightstands were smaller steamer trunks. I looked around the room, noticing the nice subway art prints on the wall and the gigantic weathered wood dresser. The guy had some serious taste.

I smiled again and closed my eyes.

"Good morning," he said and slipped into bed with me. "Still sleepy?"

"Ummm," I said. "You're up early."

"You could say that," he said and nuzzled my neck with his nose.

"Ummm," I said and loved the way he was touching me.

He spooned me and I smiled. He had only pajama bottoms on but I could feel his hard dick through them. He started rubbing up against me and I moved with him as his hands began to wander along my body, pausing to brush the hair from my shoulder to kiss the nape of my neck, taking time to squeeze my breast before going lower to my pussy lips, which he parted with his fingers and slid in, exploring me down there, taking the time to get my juices flowing. I pulled his pajama bottoms down and his dick popped out, hard and ready to fill me.

Without a word, he pulled my legs apart and stuck his cock in. We lay on our sides and made love. It was a slow process, divine and rich in feeling. And I felt it everywhere on my body. I tingled from head to toe and wanted more and more.

His hand came around and rested on my clit as he fucked me, as he took me. I began to move against it and felt the orgasm start. I moaned as his other hand squeezed my breast and pinched my nipple.

"Ahh," I moaned, really feeling so good. "I love the way you fuck me."

"Mmmm," he moaned softly in my ear. "I love to do it."

"Keep doing that," I whispered and held out for the orgasm. I didn't want this feeling to end; I wanted it to stay forever. I felt so alive yet so grounded and yet so real. It was like nothing in the world mattered but this feeling and what he was doing to me.

He kept at it, but I could tell he was holding himself back from coming and, as much I wanted to continue to do this, I couldn't help myself. It was too much. I came, the orgasm releasing millions upon millions of good tiny feelings inside of me. It was like warm sunshine just burst inside of me. I shook with it and held onto his hand, which was still between my legs. While I was still flushed with orgasm, he came, pumping into me and finding his release.

Once I was done, he was coming and pumped into me until he finished.

We didn't move for a while, only laid there and rubbed up against each other. I turned around and held him, kissing him softly and he held me tight, pulling me as close to him as he could get me.

I smiled and said, "Now, that's the best way to wake a girl up in the morning."

"I'll say," he said. "You hungry?"

"I could eat," I said but didn't want him to go.

"Then I'll fix us something," he said and gave me a kiss on the cheek and left the bed. He adjusted his pajama bottoms then pointed to the dresser. "I've got you something to wear," he said. "They're big but they'll get you back to the hotel."

I smiled as he left the room and glanced at the clothes—a super old but super comfy looking t-shirt and a pair of jean cutoffs. My panties and bra, which were now clean and fresh smelling, were folded neatly on top. I slipped them on, then the big t-shirt and then the shorts which almost fell off of me. I hiked them up and went out into the open living area. It was nice. The kitchen was at the back and the cabinets were dark wood and the appliances stainless steel. The floor looked really old, but I could tell it was refurbished oak from an old house or barn somewhere and very, very expensive. The couch was a vintage brown leather Chesterfield and the coffee table was an old looking wood box thing piled high with vintage coffee table books.

He didn't have a dining table. He had a peninsula built out and four cool looking wood stools under them for seating. The counter was a slab of concrete and so trendy and beautiful I almost asked him to marry me.

"I love your condo," I said. "When can I move in?"

He chuckled and said, "Today," with slight sarcasm and grinned at me.

"No, seriously, this is the coolest place ever."

"Thanks," he said and flipped an omelet onto a plate. "But I can't take credit for it. An old girlfriend helped me. She's an interior decorator. As for everything else, the place was pretty much already done when I moved in."

"And old girlfriend?"

He nodded. "Yeah. We're still friends. Are you friends with your ex?"

"Are you crazy?" I asked.

He chuckled and said, "Maybe a little," then slid a steaming plate of food in front of me.

It was an omelet. A steak and cheese and mushroom omelet. I looked at him. "This is my favorite kind."

"Mine, too," he said.

"Seriously?"

"Yup," he said.

"Look at us," I said. "We have something in common besides sex."

He threw his head back and laughed loudly. "But that's not a bad thing to have in common, is it?"

"Not when it's that good, baby," I told him then checked myself. *Baby?* I just called him baby! I never said stuff like this! And I certainly never flirted like this either. But it was him; he was bringing all this out in me. Maybe it there the whole time and I just had to meet the right man to bring it out. I froze. The right man? Had I lost my mind? Yes, I had. I had to keep in mind that this was just a little sex. And he was a stripper. He'd probably done this dozens of times. It was probably a routine with him by now. I knew the drill without even ever having gone through it: He'd fucked me. Now he was feeding me. Next he'd tell me it was okay to keep the clothes. And, lastly, he'd send me on my way. He wasn't about to get involved with the likes of me, a person who didn't even live in the same city as he did.

But if only... No. I stopped myself.

"How's the omelet?" he asked.

I picked up the fork and took a bite and it melted like butter in my mouth. "Oh, my God!" I moaned. "That is delicious!"

He grinned. "I make the best. We use my recipe at the diner."

"The one I saw you at last night?" I asked curiously.

He nodded. "Yeah, I own it. It's mine. Well, I own it with a business partner."

My mouth dropped. Not only was he a stripper, but he was an entrepreneur, too? Wow. Was he, like, real? I mean, I'd never come across a man like this if he wasn't in some romantic comedy or something. It was a little weird. I *felt* a little weird. And he could cook! WTF!

"So, let me get this straight," I said. "You own a diner *and* you are a stripper?"

"I own the showcase, too," he said. "But I'll retire in a few years. I can't do this much longer. I'm in my thirties now."

"But you're a stripper," I said, thinking he was skewing my whole view of the world. Weren't strippers supposed to be, like, bad with money and not exactly intelligent? Where had I heard that? Had I heard that or just made assumptions? I didn't know. The next thing I knew, he would tell me he was doing this to pay for college.

"I got into it to pay for college," he said.

I almost fell out of my chair.

"But then I realized I liked it and the money is great," he said. "And I figured out if I saved some money, I could have a house. So I saved and bought this condo. I would have built up equity, too, if only the housing market was worth a shit now."

I just stared at him. Was he for real?

"Then I began to understand that I was working for someone and they were making all the money while I did all the work. So, I formed my own dance company. We do gigs all over the country and even some outside the country, too. Australian girls love us."

I just stared at him again. How was I supposed to respond to that? I couldn't think of anything so I said, "I've always wanted to go to Australia."

He pointed at me and winked. "Next time we go, you can come with me."

Come with him? I couldn't help but glance at the door. What was going on? Had I entered the *Twilight Zone* or something? This guy was acting like... Well, like he liked me. I mean, I know he *liked* me, I just didn't think he *liked* me.

"Australia is so cool," he said. "The Great Barrier Reef? Oh, you have to see that!"

Was he going to take me? I checked him out. He was acting like he really wanted me to go with him. So I got a free trip out of this? WTF? No, seriously, what the fuck?

"But, yeah," he said, leaning on the counter. "I had to be smart, my parents taught me that. I told them I was a stripper and after they got over the shock and realized they couldn't change my mind, they told me to save that money and invest it. I did. I've been smart with my investments, too. I mean, I want to have plenty for when I have a family, you know? I want to get married and have kids. Don't you?"

I was going to pass out. I had never had a guy talk about marriage within the first twenty-four hours of meeting them. In fact, most avoided it like the plague, like if they spoke of it, I'd be all over them, begging them to marry me. Sure, they were assholes, but still. This was the reason my ex and I broke up. He didn't want to get married. But then, maybe that was because there was something wrong with him. He was a few years older than me and still running around like he was in his early twenties, going to bars and trying to pick up women. In a few years, he was going to look pathetic. But me? What about me? How did I look? I didn't know.

"Myra?" he said. "What about you? Don't you want to get married?"

"You're not for real, Cold Hard Cash," I told him.

"What do you mean?"

"You're just not real."

"Are you saying I'm fronting?"

"Are you?"

"I am not," he said.

"Listen, I want to have more sex with you," I said. "You don't have to work me."

He bristled at my words. "Work you? What the fuck does that mean?"

What was I saying? And why was I ruining this? What was wrong with me? Why even bother calling him out for playing me when I was leaving in…what? Two days? I thought about that and got a sick feeling. I didn't really want to leave. But I couldn't stay, that much was obvious.

Just then my phone rang. We stared at each other, then he straightened up and retrieved my clutch from the coffee table and handed it me. I pulled my phone out and answered, "Hello."

"Where the fuck are you?!" Becca shrieked in my ear. "We're getting ready to call Miami Metro!"

"Oh, fuck! Oh, shit!" I said and looked at Cash. What the hell could I tell her? Well, why not the truth? I measured my words and said, "I… Well, it's like… First of all, I'm okay and thanks for the concern."

"Where the fuck are you!"

"I'm with Cash."

A long pause. A very long pause.

"Are you there?" I asked.

"Are you serious?" she asked.

"I am," I said.

She sighed with relief and said, "Well, okay then. We got up late and we thought you were sleeping in and then we went and looked and your bed hadn't been slept in and… You get the picture." She paused and yelled to Nicki, "She's with Cash! Yeah, Cash! Cold! Hard! Cash!"

Nicki came on the phone, "Are you fucking serious? You boned him?"

"Well, he boned me," I said and glanced at him. He stood back, leaning against the counter with his arms crossed. He didn't like me talking about him like this, like he was a piece of meat. He was angry. I was an idiot.

"Jealous!" she squealed. "I am so jealous! Does he have a big...? You know, a big dick?"

"He does," I said. "Maybe we can talk about that later?"

"Oh, every last detail," she said. "I am going to live vicariously though you, okay?"

"Okay," I said a little uncertainly. "Listen, I'll talk to you later."

"Congrats, bitch!" she squealed. "You fucked the best one!"

"Bye," I said and laughed a little, then hung up. I set the phone down and stared at him. What now?

"You should go," he said and wouldn't look at me.

"Come on," I said.

"No," he said. "You should go."

"Why? Why should I go?"

He shook his head with frustration. "This is why I don't date! This is why I don't get involved. No one can handle it. I was stupid for thinking that you would be any different. I thought you were different."

Ouch. That hurt. But I understood where he was coming from. I got it. I had been stupid, short-sighted. I had assumed that because he was a stripper he'd be *that* kind of guy, the kind that used women and then booted them out. But he wasn't that guy at all. He was actually a man. A real man. And just because his job might be a little sketchy to some, it made him no less of a man.

"Just leave," he said.

"Come on," I said again. "It's just that you're so..." I stared at him, looking all sad and said, "You're so hot."

"So are you!" he said, his voice rising. "I told you that you were the most beautiful woman in the room last night."

"I thought you just said that to all the girls."

"No, I don't," he said. "I don't say that to just anyone. Just you."

I didn't know how to respond to that. But I did say, "Just me?"

"Just you," he said. "I thought you were different."

Why did he keep saying that? It was a little cold. Why was he getting so riled up about all this? It's not like we... No, it wasn't like we had a future together or anything. This was just fun, an affair. Right?

"But, no!" he said and threw his hands up in frustration. "You're like all the rest! You think I'm just some piece of meat."

Well, yeah. I stared at him, looking so serious and burst into laughter. This intensity he was displaying made him that much hotter. And he was already smokin'! He glared at me. I held my hands up and said, "I'm sorry, but I just can't take you seriously right now. You're just too fucking sexy!"

"Oh, my God," he said. "I can't believe *you* right now."

"Sorry, sorry," I said. "I don't think you're just some piece of meat."

"Well, I'm not," he said. "That's my job. And, get this, I love my job. Aaron, the jackhammer guy, is married with three kids and he works hard to give his family the life they want. What is so wrong with a man doing what he has to do to provide for his family? Nothing! At the end of the day, it's about money, Myra. Money."

He was right about that. It was just I'd never thought about it, and I'd certainly never been put in this situation before. But could it be possible that I'd met the rare man who wanted to get married, have a family and lead a normal life? Could it be possible? But it wasn't normal; he was a stripper. How would I tell my parents? "Mom, Dad, I am going to marry a stripper." They'd freak out. And my sister? God, I dreaded that conversation. But I was getting way ahead of myself. He didn't want to marry me and I didn't know about marrying him. This was supposed to be fun! Why had it suddenly turned not fun?

"But I know what you're getting at," he said, pointing his finger at me.

"What?"

"Nothing," he said. "I don't have to explain myself to some girl I just met."

"Some girl?" I asked, almost seething. Was he serious?

"That's right," he said. "Oh, let me guess. You dated some asshole who—surprise, surprise—didn't want to get married. So now you think all men are like that and can't understand when one isn't. You come in here with your preconceived notions and judge me. Guess what? I am not one of those assholes!"

"I never said you were an asshole!"

"Why do you think all those women come to our shows? To get loaded and grab some ass? Well, some of them do, but some they come because we're a fantasy to them and for a night we give them what they all want—a fantasy man. They're like you, women who can't meet a good man."

"Like me?" I asked, shocked. "I'm not looking for a man! I'm on vacation!"

"Well, get back to it," he said and went to the front door and opened it. "We could have had something. You and I, we could have had something."

"But you're a stripper!" I said, almost laughing.

His face dropped. Oh, fuck me and my big mouth! I hadn't meant it like that! I mean... I didn't know how to take him.

"Oh, is that all I am?" he snapped.

"I didn't mean it like that," I pleaded. "Please understand that this isn't the sort of relationship situation I'm used to."

"Why?" he asked, staring me dead in the eye. "Because it could actually work?"

I blanched. "That was a little below the belt, Cash."

"And you don't hit below the belt with your comments about me being a stripper? Huh?"

I sighed heavily and wanted to move away from him. This was too heavy, too much. It was supposed to be fun!

"So what I do is holding you back?" he asked, then paused for thought. "Well, I'm a person just like everybody else and if you can't accept me and what I do for a living, then you can't have me."

I stared at him. I couldn't have him? Not even right now? Not even just for a little while? I was leaving soon and I thought this was just a fling. I mean, the guy had a lot of things going for him. But could he be for real? I didn't know. It was too good to be true and when something is too good to be true, it usually isn't.

I stared at him, then at the door. Then I went to the door and shut it, facing him. I wasn't leaving and he couldn't make me. There was something to this man and I wanted more. He was going to let me in. I was going to see to that. And so what if I was leaving? So what if there was baggage here? Right now we were together. We might not have that in a few days. Right now, I was making the decision to be with him and he could go along for the ride. He liked me, I was sure of that, and I liked him. We had today and tomorrow. After that, we'd have to see.

He told me to leave, once more, almost begging me with his eyes. I could see that he had been hurt before by people like me and he had made a real effort to let me in. Now he'd been hurt again and wanted me to leave. I was so sorry for my small-minded assumptions. They had made an ass out of me. But I didn't want to leave. I wanted to stay and I wanted him to want me to stay.

I wanted him. There was something magnetizing about him and I was stuck having to do what my heart told me to do. And my lust, too. And I was staying and he was going to fuck me again. Later on, we could work this out, or not, but right now, we were going to have sex.

And so, I told him to do it, to fuck me, to take me, to give me all he had. He'd hesitated but then he was overcome by his emotions, by his lust and he took me, fucked me against the wall, giving me himself, all of himself and I gave him myself, too. When it was over, he held me tight. In that moment, I knew it was going to be hard to let him go.

☙

Cash took me all over Miami, showing me everything the city had to offer. I called the girls and told them I was in lust and that I wanted to spend time with him. They said they understood but we did have to catch a plane in a few days. I kept putting off reality until one morning I got a text that read: "Pln lvs in 3 hrs HURRY! Bec."

I panicked. Cash was sitting beside me on a park bench, staring out over the ocean. He looked so cool and handsome I wanted to cry. It was over. It was time to leave. I had to go back home and get back to my life, my boring life. And we'd had so much fun. We'd had our argument and then we refused to talk about it, like anyone with any sense would.

He glanced over my shoulder and read the text, then sighed. "Well."

I stared at him and wanted to beg him to beg me to stay. We'd had some great sex and such a good time I hated to see it end.

I started to get sad when he said, "Maybe we could—"

"Let's don't," I said and took his hand and squeezed it. "If it's meant to be, then we'll know. Right?"

He nodded. "I suppose."

I stared at him and knew the wheels were turning inside his head. He was a deep thinker, that was for sure. So,

I said, "If you think about something too much, Cash, it ruins it."

He threw his head back and laughed, then shook it at me. "You are adorable. You're a pain in the ass, but you are adorable."

"So, I'm an adorable pain in the ass?"

"You are."

Good to know.

But the fact was, reality was setting in and I knew that this might not work. We were in the throes of passion and sometimes that makes you a fool. I'd know when I got back home what to do. It was killing me to leave, but I had no choice.

He dropped me off at my hotel and I got on the elevator, went to my room and packed. Becca and Nicki had already gone to the airport, texting me that they'd meet me there to say goodbye and then they'd go to their gate and I'd go to mine. We were on separate flights this time. There was no real reason why they should fly back to Atlanta with me.

I didn't think about what I was doing; I just did it. I took a cab to the airport and then started the check-in process. The whole time, I kept wanting to look over my shoulder for him, but I refused. The real reason was because I believed I'd just been a fling for him. That's all I'd been. And I knew if he didn't come, then we were finished. It would be a fantastic memory but that's all it would be.

I made it to security and got in line to go through. Then I thought I might need to text Becca and Nicki to see if they were boarding yet as I wanted to see them before they left. But then, for some reason, I paused and glanced over my shoulder. Just that once.

And there he was. Cold. Hard. Cash. Not so cold, not so hard. He was walking towards me with purpose. He was showing me that I had made the right decision. He'd let me go but then realized he couldn't let me leave and that made me the happiest girl in the whole wide world. I had my man now! And he was such a good, good man. Even if his career choice was a little questionable.

"You didn't think I was just going to let you go, did you?" he asked as he walked towards me.

I kinda had. But I was so glad he'd proved me wrong.

He stopped in front of me and then shook his head, wiping the tears from my face with the back of his hand. "No, no crying. That's not allowed in Miami."

I laughed and tiptoed to kiss him and he kissed back, showing me that there was something between us and it was this incredible love I'd given up on, had lost hope on, didn't believe existed. It *did* exist. This was it. Right here, in front of me, kissing me back and telling me that while fairy tales aren't real, you can certainly tweak reality and start to believe in true love.

My parents would say I was crazy. My sister would roll her eyes. The women I worked with would be so jealous. But my best friend, Becca, and even my new best friend, Nicki, would tell me, right to my face, "You did good, girl."

And they'd be right.

Love Hurts

"Are you serious?" I asked him in disbelief.

He didn't say a word.

"Gil?" I said, this short of getting infuriated. But that's what he wanted. He wanted me mad, angry. He wanted me flailing around like a crazed animal. This was so he could take control of the situation and show me who the man was, who was the boss. He wanted to show me so bad.

I wasn't having it.

Without a word, I got up and crossed the room to the front door. Once I reached it, he was there, barring my way. We hadn't had sex yet but since the day I met him, I knew we would. But not now. I hated him at that moment. I wanted him to leave and I never wanted to lay eyes on him again.

"Where you going?" he asked.

I could have slapped him but I didn't. I restrained myself, gained control of my feelings and said calmly, "*I'm* not going anywhere. You're the one who's leaving. It's late and I need to go to bed."

He leaned back and gave me the once over. "Can't take it, can you, Mina?"

"Please get out," I said but didn't open the door.

"Can't take it," he said mockingly. "Can dish it out, but she can't take it."

I hated men like him. I hated them pushing my buttons. I hated succumbing to these feelings of hatred, irritation and frustration. But that's what we did to each other, men like him, women like me; we succumbed to the hate and then, as we clawed through the hate, we got to the love. It was a long, tiring process. It was enough to drive anyone insane.

"Shut the fuck up," I said, infuriated.

"Such a pretty girl," he said. "But a mouth like a sailor."

"I wouldn't know," I said dryly. "I don't know any sailors."

He laughed, loving my smart mouth. His eyes scanned over me, taking me in, almost consuming me. He liked what he saw. He liked it a lot. He liked the curves set in my petite frame. He liked my dark brown hair and bright blue eyes. He liked the spray of freckles on my chest, which he'd commented on before. He liked me, it was that simple.

I didn't know if I wanted to return the favor.

"I'm sure you don't know any sailors," he said and grinned at me.

He was so getting on my nerves. So bad. Why didn't he just leave? It wasn't supposed to be like this. But what it was supposed to be like was beyond my comprehension. What were we even doing together? We didn't know each other that well. We'd only just met a few weeks or so ago and had only been on a few dates since. We'd met at a mutual friend's engagement party and he had asked me if I was married. I had told him no, I wasn't. In fact, I'd never been married. I had been engaged though, just a few weeks ago, until my ass of a boyfriend broke up with me to run off with some hussy he'd met in a bar. No, I didn't tell him that. I didn't tell him how pissed off I'd been at first, but then, oddly enough, relieved. It was over and I was happy that I didn't have to break up with him, which I had, in fact, wanted to. Instead I told Gil I was still engaged, off limits, and to leave me alone. He told me someone had told him I wasn't engaged anymore. I didn't have a clue as to who had told him that but I was irritated at them for it.

But the fact was, I was intimidated by him. I really didn't want him to know anything about me, lest he try to use it against me later, lest he try to manipulate me into something. I had tried to stop whatever it was we might have before its inception, but had been unsuccessful. And so, here we were, after an awkward date, fighting like we'd been married for years. It was odd. We had this kinetic energy that seemed to get under our skins and drive us crazy.

Why I had agreed to go out with him in the first place was beyond me. Perhaps I was a glutton for punishment.

I couldn't help but wonder what the sex would be like, though. The other day, after yet another disastrous date, he'd come back here to my apartment and found a riding crop I had left in the corner of the living room. He asked me why I had one of these. I'd told him I rode, of course, and kept my horse at a nearby stable. It was one of my biggest pleasures, riding. He went over and picked the crop up and said, "Ever thought of doing something else with this?" I immediately knew he meant—something sexual—and was flooded with embarrassment. I didn't know what exactly he would do with the crop, but I knew enough that it would be just a little kinky. And I wasn't ready for kinky. I didn't know if I'd ever be ready for that. I'd had a somewhat dull sexual relationship with my ex, very vanilla and before him I'd only slept with a few other guys. So, I was a little inexperienced in that capacity.

This was probably the reason Gil and I had this strained thing going on between us. I knew he was the kind of guy to push my limits, to push me beyond my boundaries. He was so manly, such a take-charge kind of guy. But I wasn't that kind of girl. I held back too much. That's why all of this was scary to me. It was new. It was something I'd never experienced before.

He was staring at me again, his eyes not leaving me. I sighed and felt so self-conscious and just so... Well, pent up. But I wasn't having this, whatever it was he wanted to give me. I was also unsure if we'd ever be able to make this work. "I've changed my mind," I told him. "I don't want to do this anymore."

"What are you so afraid of?" he asked softly.

"Nothing," I said. "I'm not afraid of anything."

"Like hell you're not."

"Please," I said, hating the sound of my voice, just this short of begging. "Please just get out."

"Why?" he said. "Why don't you want it?"

I looked away in embarrassment. I didn't know. We'd been so close just a few minutes ago and I'd turned it off. *Just like that.* I mean, I did want it but there was this conflict I had. I had a hard time trusting, that's all. And I had a hard time trusting Gil. I knew he'd be a good lover, better than any I'd had before him. However... Well, I just couldn't seem to take that initial yet so crucial step to get to the sex.

"It's not right," I said. "I'm engaged."

He chuckled. "Playing that card, are you? You know I know it's not true."

I blanched. He was right. Yeah, we were, we were broken up, my ex and I. I was a free woman, more or less. But free from what? And to do what? I didn't know and didn't care to analyze what that might mean. But then, I shivered with shame, thinking of all the personal details of my life that I'd lain out on the table for him to pore over, to dissect, to use against me later. I should have played my cards a little closer to my vest.

"Come on," he said. "You know you want it."

And that was the problem. I did want it and I wanted it from him. And here I was, presented with the perfect opportunity to get it and all I could do was run away. It was like having a crush on someone then getting the chance to talk to them, but you can't. You stutter and stammer and make a damn fool out of yourself. Then they see you, they see the need in you and they run, don't they? They always run away from it, from that need, lest they lose themselves in it. They were afraid of giving themselves up to the love, to *your* love. They're afraid of losing themselves in your need. That's why they always made it so hard. It was a battleground, love. And everyone wanted to fight.

That's when I got it. I finally understood. Love hurts. It hurts a lot. Even if you're no longer in love with the person who hurt you. It hurts and makes fools of people, just like the fool I'd become when my ex dumped me. Even if I didn't care and even if I didn't really want him anymore, I had been hurt by it. Rejection was a terrible thing. It made people insecure and question themselves. It can shut them off from the world, too, from new love entering because they might just be afraid of what will happen if they succumb to it again. Could we chance getting hurt again? Why was there always the threat of ensuing pain when love came into the picture? That the pain always seemed to be inevitable? I wasn't sure and for that, I hesitated, though the hesitation was killing me. I wanted to move forward but I didn't know how. But I knew that this was a big obstacle for me. I wasn't looking for love right then but I knew it might have just landed in my lap with Gil. I was afraid of it, afraid of the way he looked at me, like he felt something. And he did. I felt it, too. But it was too soon after my breakup.

We'd have to try this again later. He'd just have to understand. So, I tried to push past him but he wouldn't let me open the door so he could, then, step through it and leave. I stepped back and crossed my arms, glaring at him. Why wouldn't he just go? I wanted him to leave so I could make a plan about what to do with my life now and somehow, get wrapped back up in my security, the security which was now evading me. I felt insecure not knowing what I was going to do. But I knew one thing for sure and that was I wasn't going to continue this...this...whatever this was he and I had. This just wouldn't work out. This was too much for me. I couldn't handle it, these mind games. I just wanted him to go. *Why wouldn't he just go?*

But I knew the answer to this. It was because he knew why I'd invited him here in the first place and it certainly wasn't for coffee and stimulating conversation. He knew I wanted to get fucked and he wanted to fuck me. The problem was that I was too inhibited. I had trouble asking for sex, even admitting I wanted it to myself. I just couldn't cross that line to get what I wanted. Of course, he was going to let me get what I wanted and that was because he more than wanted to give it to me, if only I could just open myself up to allow it. That was the problem, getting past the self-consciousness and onto the sex. But I'd always been like that, even with my ex. That might have been why we broke up. He wanted sex all the time and I didn't. I was content to just read a book or watch TV. He was a pushover though and he let me have it my way. We rarely had sex and when we did, it wasn't that spectacular. But Gil? Well, he was different. He wanted sex and wasn't afraid to let me know that he wanted it. Besides that, he wasn't a pushover. Moreover, he liked to play games, mind games. I almost think he just loved to torment me in that way. It gave him a kick to wind me up and watch me go crazy. I suppose it would be entertaining for him if I did.

"Just one kiss," he said. "Come on. Let's just try it. Just one kiss."

Just one kiss... But I knew that one would lead to two and I was terrified of three. I wasn't built for this, for this strong sexual attraction, for this need. But he made me want him. He was tall and muscular. He was handsome; his dark hair lightened by the sun and his skin tanned by it. He was a man, pure and simple, and that meant he was strong. I was a woman. Did that make me weak? I knew I was weakened by these games we played.

"It's supposed to be fun," I muttered.

"It is fun," he replied. "We just have to get through this awkward part."

He was waiting on me, waiting me out. He was being patient. He was willing to help me through this, to take me to the other side. But I didn't know why it was so hard for me to just *do* it. Why was it so hard? Why did I feel the need to cover it up and pretend I didn't have it this need? And the need was for sex, pure and simple. I wanted sex. I just couldn't allow myself to admit I wanted it. And I couldn't allow him to see how much I wanted it. But I did want it and I wanted to feel the satisfaction from having it. So, why couldn't I go through with it? With the sex? What was the big deal? It was just sex. I was a free woman; it was okay if I fucked him. But something in me held me back, kept me subdued, kept me from getting what I wanted.

"Come on, Mina," he muttered and stepped in closer to me. "Come on, just one kiss."

Just one kiss... Just one. That's all. One kiss. Why not? Why not just one kiss? What could it hurt? I was afraid of letting go, that's all, of trusting, of getting hurt again. And I knew that if I allowed Gil in and he hurt me, it would kill me. I already felt more for him than I ever had for my ex. That's what scared me, that's what held me back. It was causing my erratic behavior. It was blocking me and would not let me through. And it was just fear, plain and simple. I was too afraid to go through with it, the sex. I was too afraid of falling in love again. The sex would cement our attraction and then... Well, I couldn't really handle another breakup any time soon. I, simply, didn't want to get hurt.

He was waiting. He was waiting on me. This was it. Do it, do it now, get it over with. And so I did. No more holding back, driving myself crazy. This was it. Now. Do it now.

He was still waiting. Would he wait forever? I doubted it. He would soon grow bored with me, with this little goody-goody act I had. But I wasn't a goody-goody. Not really. Never had been. So why could I not just cross that line and get what I wanted? And what I wanted was to be fucked by him, this handsome man who had, more or less, been waiting patiently on me. I realized he wasn't the one playing games, I was. That made me feel embarrassed. That made me realize I was acting like a fool, like an idiot. It made me want to do it, to take what he was offering me. I knew our sex wouldn't be the "slam, bam, thank you ma'am" variety. I knew he had something up his sleeve and the thought of letting him do whatever he wanted to do to me made me more than just a little nervous. But what would he do to me? It was as intriguing as it was scary. Maybe I should... No. I wasn't going to play that game again. I was going to get what I wanted. And so, yes, it was time. But could I do it? I could. Surely, I could. I just had to have some faith in myself; I had to have some trust in Gil. I had to let go of the fear of him hurting me. And I had to fuck him. I had to do it. It was the only way to get through this block. This was what men and women do, right? I could do it, too.

"Mina?" he said. "What's next?"

"I don't know," I said, leaving it up to him. "You figure it out."

"Does that mean that you trust me?"

I thought about that and nodded in the affirmative. I did. I trusted him. I said, "Yes. I trust you."

He smiled. I couldn't smile back. I was too nervous. And I wanted it. I wanted him to do it and do it quickly so I could end this madness. I was in such a twist about everything since my breakup I didn't know what to do or how to think. Maybe this was too soon, but then again, I couldn't stay by myself for an eternity. And I wasn't saving myself for any sort of future relationship. I had to live in the moment and the moment right now dictated that I fuck Gil. He was the best bet to get me over this barrier.

"Yes, Gil," I said. "You can do whatever you like."

He smiled. He liked that idea. He came over to me, bending down a little and took my face in his hands. I allowed him to look into my eyes and then let him brush his lips against mine. Shivers went up and down my spine and I began to panic and want to run away again. But there was no going back. No going back after this. I was sick of going back. I just wanted to go forward.

"Gil," I said and pushed him away. "I just—"

He wouldn't let me finish. He shook his head. "You said you trusted me."

I had said that.

"So be quiet," he demanded.

I nodded and stopped talking, thinking, reacting. I was headed into the moment. I knew that's where I was going and I was going fast. No stopping now.

"Relax," he said. "We'll take it slow."

I nodded and allowed him to walk me back though the living room and into the bedroom. I allowed him to push me down on the bed and then... Then I felt so stupid, like a virgin. Maybe I was a virgin again. I hadn't been with another man since the day I'd met my boyfriend, nearly five years ago, when I was only twenty-six. That was a long time to spend with just one man. Wasn't it?

"Close your eyes," he said.

I closed my eyes and bit my bottom lip.

"Now just relax," he said and began to caress my body. "God, you're so beautiful. Anyone ever told you that?"

I nodded. Yeah, I'd gotten that line a few times. Once I was at a party and a guy was flirting with me. After a while, he leaned back and said, "You're very beautiful." It made me nervous, though, and made me wonder why he had done such a thing, mostly because I had gone to the party with my ex-boyfriend and I was more than sure he had come with a date. But I just shrugged it off and excused myself, feeling slightly odd. Fact was, I rarely felt beautiful. I knew I looked good, but I was never comfortable with it. I wanted to be comfortable with it. I wanted to show the world I liked who I was and I liked the way I looked. It was a hard thing for me to do, though.

But Gil wanted me to feel it. He wanted me to feel beautiful. He was taking his time to undress me. My shirt was now on the floor. Then he was pushing his hand across my chest, then down to my breasts, still secure in my bra. My nipples rose up in anticipation of his mouth and I began to yearn for him. My heartbeat escalated and my breathing became faster. I could feel his hand on my breast. I could feel the need in his body. He needed this to go through. He'd been patient long enough. But... But...

I rose up on my elbows and pushed him away. He paused and stared at me, then his head dropped and I could read his thoughts: *Again? She's doing this again?* And I was. What was wrong with me? It was in there, that sexuality, and it wanted out. Why couldn't I let it out?

Without a word, he rose from the bed, staring me in the eye. I stared back, thinking he was leaving and this time for good. But I was wrong. What he did next shocked me.

He went over to my dresser and pulled out the top drawer, rummaged around then pushed it back in and went the next and then the next and then the next like he was looking for something. I started to say something, to ask him what he was doing but he held a hand up, silencing me. I didn't speak and waited to see what he was doing. Finally, he stopped. He had apparently found what he was looking for and pulled something out of the last drawer. I recognized it as a scarf I sometimes tied around my head to get that mod, sixties rich girl on a yacht look. I loved that scarf. But what was he doing with it?

I sat up as he neared the bed and waited. He leaned over and wrapped the scarf around my eyes, covering them. What was he doing? My eyes were covered. I was in the dark. He was in control. I felt a slight panic.

"Gil," I began to protest. "What are—"

"I'm done with this," he said. "Now you can either do this or I will leave. This is it, Mina. I won't try again."

"But what are you doing?" I asked. I'd never had this done to me before.

"Why don't you just trust me?" he said, growing impatient again.

Trust him? Could I? Should I? But… But…

"This is what it's going to take," he said and pushed me back on the bed. "Just go with it."

I tensed. I didn't like feeling so vulnerable, so open and raw. But then I realized something. If he was in control, then I wasn't. If he had control, then all I had to do was follow his lead. I no longer had to think about it. I could surrender control of what was going to happen. If I did that, everything might just fall into place and allow me to sate my ever growing sexual appetite for him. It was about surrender, wasn't it? Surrendering oneself to another so they could do as they pleased to you, to your body and soul. For your love, even. Surrendering yourself so that someone else could bring out the desires in you that would have otherwise stayed hidden. Was that what might come out of this? Love? Something to cherish, to hold onto, to take and to consume?

And so, I surrendered. I let him have control. The reins were in his hands now. And then… Then I heard him removing his belt. His belt. I tensed with anticipation and waited, turning my face to the side and I listened with rapt attention, trying to figure out what he was doing, what he was going to do with the belt. Then my arms were above my head and he was tying my hands together with his belt. With his belt. *What the hell?* And what could I do? All of a sudden, I didn't care. I was going with it. I began to feel something different, something tantalizing. I began to feel arousal and anticipation of what was to come. Next, my legs were tied with what I assumed was another scarf from my dresser. In less than a minute, I had been rendered submissive. Now I no longer had a choice. I had to do as he wanted.

As he wanted. And then I realized this was what he had planned all along, to get me to submit to him, to his desires. And, oddly enough, I was fine with that. I began to feel excitement then, wondering what he was going to do next. But just before I handed myself over to the experience, my good old friend insecurity showed up. And, along with it, my good old friend fear.

"Gil," I said, on the verge of panicking. "I don't like this."

"Shh," he said and covered my mouth with his hand. "Be quiet."

I sucked my bottom lip into my mouth and wanted to say something. But I didn't. I don't know what happened but all of a sudden, I knew that it was okay. I was getting so turned on, I no longer cared. I knew what he was doing and he was putting me in a position to surrender control and so I was. And all I kept thinking was: What would he do next?

He rolled me over.

His hands were all over me then, touching me, massaging me. It felt good, relaxing. Then he slipped my black pencil skirt off and threw it to the side. Now I was lying there in my underwear, feeling more than just a little vulnerable, more than just a little nervous. He'd never seen me naked before.

But he didn't make a move to take off my bra or my panties, a black lace set that showed off my trim body. No, not yet. He just stared at me. I couldn't see him staring at me as my eyes were covered, but he was. I could feel his heavy gaze and that made my heart beat even more rapidly.

"Gil," I said, wondering why he was hesitating. It was killing me, the waiting. What was he going to do next?

"One minute," he said and left the room.

"What?" I asked but he didn't respond. A minute later, he was back in the room, standing over me. Then he bent and turned me over and pushed my hips up into the air, my elbows on the bed, hands still tied. And then I felt it, a thin, leather tipped thing. It took me a second but I suddenly recognized it as my riding crop and he was moving it down my back and to my buttocks. And without a word, he gave me a good, quick tap right across the ass. I was about to say something, but then I heard him murmur, "Shhh...."

Shhhh... So, I was silent. I also burned with embarrassment as the crop tapped onto my skin. My face, my entire body was lit up. I didn't know what to do. He was, essentially, whipping me with a riding crop. And then he did it again. Harder. I felt like I should tell him to stop, to make him stop. He shouldn't be doing this to me. I wasn't ready for something like this. This was too much for me. I was way in over my head.

I opened my mouth to tell him to stop but something in me told me to wait, to see what he was going to do next. He gave me another lick and then another and then I began to feel it; I felt the tension, all the tension in my body, ease and then subside and then I began to moan loudly. And I began to tingle in anticipation. I waited, breathless, and wanted more. This was something I couldn't control and I liked the feeling. He gave me a few more licks, just slight taps, then finished it off with one solid swat that burned into my skin. I forced my face into the pillow and held back a wail. Oh, but I was loving this. I was surprised. It was odd that someone like me, someone who only enjoyed sex occasionally, would like such a thing. But that's when I realized he was doing this to get me to submit to my sexual desires and the crop was nothing more than an instrument that aided in his dominance. To let me know on a primal level that he was the boss.

I tried not to think about it. It was a little overwhelming. And, so, I just concentrated on the pleasure I felt, the freedom and the liberation that good, hot and, yes, kinky sex can give a woman.

He discarded the riding crop after that. He rubbed and then kissed the places on my skin where the crop had been, then turned me over onto my back. I lay there and drew in a breath as he climbed over me.

And he began.

He began to directly bring it out in me, this sexual being that was being held captive. His hands began to roam my body, moving over my breasts which were still in my bra and then down my stomach and then down my legs, then back up again. His hands were flat and smooth as they traced lines on my curves and as they paused to squeeze a breast.

I was there, in that moment, and I was slowly but surely coming even more alive. I could feel the tingles starting to happen and I could feel my inner being begin to allow it to happen, to want it to happen. His hands continued to explore me, my body, resting ever so often, holding still to make me move. To make me ache for it. And I began to move, to arch away from the bed, towards his body to long for his lips, for his kiss.

But he made me wait. He was making me cross that line into want. I had to want it; I had to beg for it and he was making sure I did. I had to cross that line, all while tied up and secured.

Yet, I did not let any words came from my lips, no begging, no pleading. I wasn't ready to go there yet. And, so, nothing came from him. Just silence. Just the rustle of the comforter on the bed as he moved over me.

And then... Then he did it. He was a man and he knew how to use this to get me to take what he wanted me to have. His lips were near mine, nearly grazing them, just softly, just slightly out of reach. I found myself rising up a little and trying to meet his mouth. I was itching to touch his lips, his soft and full lips, the ones that had touched mine before. He pulled away, not letting me have it, not letting me kiss him, making me want it, making me have to have it. But I was tied up and couldn't grab his face and pull it to mine. I could only lie there and try to get him to kiss me. And so I realized what he was waiting for and so I began to beg. I had to. I had no other choice.

"Please," I breathed.

He didn't respond and continued to tease me by almost meeting my lips.

"Please, Gil," I said a little louder.

But nothing. He wasn't giving into me so easily.

"Please, please, please!" I moaned. "I have to have it. Please. Give it to."

"What?" he asked. "What do you want?"

"For you to kiss me," I said, waiting and wanting. "Kiss me!"

"And then what? What do you want?"

"You," I said. "I want you. You! Kiss me!"

"And then?"

"More," I breathed. "I want you to do whatever you want to do." And I did. I wanted more than that, much, much more. It was there, right there and I had to take care of this need. "Please, just do it. Don't torment me like this."

He paused, waiting. He had gotten what he wanted and he still wasn't doing anything. What was I missing? Was I not doing something right? He had proven his dominance. He was in control. I was willing to do whatever he wanted. I was over this. I wanted to stop playing this game. I wanted him and I wanted him now.

I told him, "Fuck me. Fuck me! Now!"

And that's all it took. His lips came down hard on mine then, almost crushing me. He pushed himself on top of me and that's when I realized I'd crossed the line. I was ready to fuck. This was what he was waiting for, for me to be so ready that there was no way I could back out of it. And I was ready, so, so ready.

"Mmmm," I moaned and began to lick at his mouth, slipping my tongue in so he could suck on it then offer me his. We kissed for minutes, really, really getting into it, taking it all the way.

His mouth then began to make its way down my body, just as his hands did and this time, he took full control. He pushed my bra aside and grabbed onto a nipple, sucking it into his mouth and biting down a little. I arched from the bed and wanted to grab his head and hold it there but I couldn't. My hands were still tied. Then he was at the other breast, a nipple in his mouth, eating at it, sucking at it as his other hand grabbed the other breast and squeezed tight.

I moaned with pure pleasure, with lust, wanting him, all of him, inside of me, fucking me. But not yet; he had other ideas. His head was going down, further and further down until his nose was at the top of my panties, then his teeth were grabbing and tugging them down. My legs were squeezed tightly together as they were tied, but that didn't stop him. He was licking at me, down there, going for it. I wanted him in between my legs, sucking and licking at me.

So, he untied the scarf that was binding my legs together and pushed them apart and in one quick motion, pulled my panties off so that I was now fully exposed. And he dove in. He licked my inner thighs all the way down to my knees, then back up again. He could see that I was already wet, well, more than wet; I was literally dripping. He pressed his face in between my legs. Another moan came out of my mouth and I found myself wanting my hands in his hair, playing with it, tugging at it as he began to bite and nibble at my pussy. It was swollen, so swollen now. I couldn't take it. It felt so good and I wanted more. I was ready for much, much more. And I wanted to see him but my eyes were still covered by the scarf. When would he take that off? I wanted it off. But… Not just yet.

His fingers were playing with me, pushing inside of me. He took his time to explore me then pushed his face into my naked pussy. I could feel his breath and I could feel his mouth eating me. I shivered and began to move with him, pushing myself onto him, grinding on his face as he licked and sucked on me.

It didn't take long. There was nothing I could do but come. And I came hard, harder than I'd ever come before. It might have been all the anticipation building up to this that made me erupt like that. It could have been because he was so good at it. I didn't know what it was, but when the orgasm hit me, I was liberated. Everything ceased to matter. My body just lit up and my soul soared within me.

After that, there was no stopping me. "You have to fuck me now," I moaned, wanting to look at him. "Fuck me now."

But he stopped and asked, "Are you sure?"

I nodded.

He came to me, his mouth near mine, his hand again went between my legs and began to play. I moved with his hand, almost to orgasm as he pressed his lips to mine. I licked and sucked at his lips as his hands continued to play with my pussy. My legs opened wider and he settled between them, still clothed.

"Fuck me," I began to beg, wishing the scarf was off my eyes so I could see him. "Please, fuck me."

He moved away and I heard his zipper pull, then the sound of him pulling off his pants and underwear and his shirt. He was now naked. I wished I could have seen that as his body was trim and hard and muscular in clothes. Out of clothes, I was more than sure it looked even better. But then he was on the bed, back between my legs, his hard cock teasing me, sliding up and down before finding its way in.

I gasped from the pressure of it, from the size. I gasped from the pleasure of having it in me. It felt so new, so nice, so good. It felt *right.*

He took the scarf off my face as he fucked me and we stared into each other's eyes as we did it, his forehead pressed against mine. We didn't look away and we didn't hesitate. We were doing it and we were doing it right. We were doing what we were meant to do with one another.

We were in sync. My hips rose up off the bed and my lust just took over my whole body. I was so into it, I couldn't control myself. I wanted another orgasm and I wanted his cock to give it to me. I could feel another climax deep within me, ready to be released and his cock was going to take me to it.

He untied my hands and now they were free to roam his body as he fucked me. I felt his back, his wide and muscular back, then grabbed his face, pulling it to mine and kissing him. I had felt so constrained before but now I felt free. Now I could concentrate on what it was all about and what it was all about was the fucking.

He moaned deeply as I rode him, as I fucked him. He was trying to hold back, trying not come. He could sense the orgasm in my body, he could tell I was about to have a big one and he was doing everything in his power to ensure it. He held on, he held me tight as I finally found the groove which would take me to heaven. Nothing mattered then. Nothing in the world mattered but doing this and getting it. I had to have it. It was coming and I could feel it, deep inside. It was making my legs numb and my heart beat fiercely. It was making me hot and sweaty, the effort of doing it, of not being able to stop. It was making me strong.

It was making him weak. He was about to burst. He was about to come.

Then I felt it. It started slow but built fast. It was coming strong. It was fierce and it was love and it was desire and it was all the things in the world I'd always wanted. It was mine! I grabbed onto it and a wail came out of me that I couldn't control. Then he began to really fuck me and that helped me hold onto it longer. It was a big one, a big orgasm. It took me over and then handed me myself back. Then it dissolved slowly and left me feeling weak but so satisfied.

He was pumping into me. He was coming. He was coming fast and hard with everything he had. I grabbed onto him and held him tight as he came inside me and shivered as it filled me up. He shivered, too, then kept pumping until there was nothing left, nothing left to do but fall on me and hold me tight, like he was never going to let me go.

The first thought in my mind was, *Why had I held back so much?* I knew that I'd denied myself pleasure and that wasn't right. But then it didn't matter and I couldn't help but smile. Yeah, it had been that good. It was everything I'd expected, everything I'd wanted. And I'd wanted it for so long. I'd needed it, too. Now I had it. And there was no going back. What had been the big deal? What was I so afraid of? It was more than spectacular. It had been everything I ever allowed myself to want. And I wanted more.

I lay there and listened to the ticking of the alarm clock on the nightstand and felt very, very satisfied. This was what it was all about. It was just fucking. It was just sex, getting off. It was about him dominating me and me submitting. It was about being contained so I could fly free. It was fun. It was so much fun. I wanted to do it again and again.

"How do you feel?" he asked and kissed my shoulder.

I turned to stare into his eyes, so deep blue and said, "I feel great. It's just what I needed. You were right about that."

He nodded. "Told you."

After he left, I wondered, *What have I gotten myself into?* I felt a surge of excitement combined with the dread of the unknown. But that didn't stop me from wanting him to come back soon. And quickly. I knew I was falling for him, fast and hard. I knew I was being vulnerable and that I might get hurt. But I had to do it. I had to succumb. I had no choice. Love might hurt but I knew that living without this man would be absolutely unbearable.

You, Me and Him

Something like this was bound to happen.

It started out as an innocent fascination. He was my boyfriend's best friend, of course. I mean, how else would this have come about if I hadn't known him already? And my boyfriend, too, of course.

I first met him at the club I was working at. I was DJing part-time and he came in with my boyfriend one night. I loved DJing. I loved pumping out the beats for the hoards of people that would come into the large club. I loved watching them bump and grind and dirty dance to the tunes I rocked. It was fun. It was sexy. The whole atmosphere would become so lust-filled and wanton. I just loved playing my part in it by providing the music.

We'd never met. I knew about him, of course. My boyfriend had talked about Milo for years before he actually came into the city. He lived out on the East Coast. They'd kept in constant contact and kept promising to one day meet up and have a wild time. They'd been best friends since summer camp and blah, blah, blah. Toby told me, "You'd love him, Holly. He's cool and really funny. I can't wait for you to meet him."

Cool and really funny didn't begin to cover it. Milo was the epitome of masculinity and if a person looked as good as he did, cool and funny could take a back seat, though having it all—looks, humor and coolness—wasn't anything to sneeze at. Milo was tall, dark and handsome. Sea green eyes and short black hair. Ummm... He looked so good I could have eaten him up. I mean, I'd seen pictures of him before, but seeing him in live Technicolor glory was enough to floor a girl. I kept thinking, "Why isn't he taken? Why isn't this guy married or at the very least, in a long term relationship?" Well, he had been and it hadn't worked out, as he told me later. As a result, he was taking a break. Let me tell you, I wouldn't have minded if that break included me.

Then again, I was in a relationship. With my boyfriend. For several years. It wasn't like I could jump Milo's bones, though, I have to admit, I would have. If I could have had a free pass for just one guy, he would have been it. And I mean I-T, it!

Nevertheless, that was neither here nor there. I was in no position to even consider sleeping with him. I was in love. My boyfriend was a catch. He owned his own recording studio and surfed religiously, which kept his lean body ripped and his sandy blonde hair highlighted. He was also cool. He was tall and so cute I wanted to pinch his cheeks. He treated me like a princess. He helped me get the DJing gig I had always wanted. He was everything a girl could want and more.

So, why did Milo catch my eye and hold it? Well, he was spectacular, too. He'd been an investment banker and, once the market crashed, had decided to do what he loved best which was playing guitar. He'd told Toby that being an investment banker had been soul draining for him and he wanted something different. Toby told him to come out West, that he could always use good studio musicians. He told him that he needed to live a little in the sunshine and get his mind off the hustle and bustle of high finance. We were only a short walk to the beach and they could surf and grab a taco from a stand. He didn't give Milo much of a choice. It was a wonderful opportunity Toby was offering his best friend. So, why not?

Maybe because his girlfriend has a bad case of the wandering eye? *That's* why not. But that's all it was, a wandering eye. I wasn't a cheater in any sense of the word. When I was in a monogamous relationship, I stayed monogamous. It was that simple. But I did like to look. What woman doesn't?

But why did I have to pick between them? Was it possible I could have both? Probably not. Not many women get that lucky. I didn't think I would either. This didn't keep me from fantasizing about Milo, though. And those fantasizes led to some amazing sex with Toby. And I mean ah-mazing! By the time we got though with one another, all we could do was lie on our backs, stare at the ceiling and try to catch our breaths.

"That was fantastic," Toby said and exhaled loudly. "What's gotten into you?"

Like I could divulge that bit of information.

∞

The night I met Milo for the first time was at the club. I was up on the podium laying down some wicked beats when I glanced down and saw him. I had no idea who he was at the time. He was new to me. And looked so damned good. Who was this guy? And how could I meet him?

At once, our eyes clicked. I think my heart skipped a beat. Again: *Who was this guy?* He stared back at me with a mixture of curiosity and interest. There was a connection, it was obvious. I felt it and I knew he felt it. We were strangers but somehow we were connected.

From the intense gaze this good looking stranger was giving me, I could feel his fantasies about me taking shape. I could tell he liked what he saw. I was hot. I stood there with my light brown hair pulled back into a loose ponytail, my sun-kissed skin gleaming and my blue eyes meeting his. His eyes scanned over me, over my outfit of loose fitting black tank over a tighter fitting white one and my worn to death and perfectly fitted skinny jeans. He took a look at my black leather ankle boots and the mixture of bracelets on my arm and then he looked back at my face, to the headphones I was holding over one ear. Back down to my breasts which were slightly popping out of the fitted tank. I could feel his eyes there, on my breasts and I imagined him wanting to pinch a nipple before sucking it into his mouth. It was enough to make me go wet, that stare. It was enough for me to want to find him, get to know him better and fuck his brains out.

Then I saw Toby step in beside him and yell something in his ear. They both laughed and Toby pointed to the stage and pointed at me. We knew at once who the other was. The reaction showed on our faces as Milo's face fell, as did mine. The guy I'd been having wild fantasies about was Milo, my boyfriend's best friend. It was over before it could have ever started.

Of fucking course.

He was off limits to me and vice versa. Whatever lust or connection we had felt was now null and void. There would be no quickies in the bathroom or even a mild flirtation. There would never be an "us" because there was a Toby and, truth be told, that's the way it should have been. We both loved Toby and wouldn't have hurt him for the world. He was too good of a guy and if you hurt someone like Toby, then you would just be a bad person.

Soon enough, my time was up and another DJ took over. I made my way over to the bar. Toby glanced over his should just as I came up and broke into a big smile. He was so happy to see me; I could see the love in his eyes. So, yeah, no. There would be no Milo and me.

"Hey, baby," Toby said and slipped his arm around my waist, giving me a quick peck on the cheek. "This is the famous Milo."

I held out my hand to him and said, "I've heard so much about you. It's nice to finally meet."

"Oh, you have an accent," he said and gave my hand a quick shake. "Southern?"

"Born and raised," I said and smiled at him.

"Well, nice to meet you," he said and withdrew his hand.

And that was that. I noticed he wasn't saying much, let alone looking at me. I knew why. He didn't want Toby to think that he might be interested in me. Well, I could play that game, too. I didn't want him to think I was interested in him, either. We could play it straight. We *would* play it straight. No funny business, even if he was one of the best looking men I'd ever laid eyes on.

"He just got into town," Toby said and pointed at him. "And he drove to the house." He paused to punch him on the arm in a good-natured way. "I told you I'd pick you up at the airport!"

"It wasn't a big deal," Milo said. "Besides I had already booked my rental car."

I nodded. "Well, at least you made it though the traffic."

"I did," he said and avoided my eyes. "But I'm used to it. New York traffic is hell. But then again, I rarely drive in it. I usually take a cab or the subway. I don't even own a car."

"Parking is a killer, right?" I said, trying to make friendly conversation.

"It is," he said. "And expensive. A car just isn't practical for a lot of people."

God, what a monotonous conversation, I thought to myself. Was this what it would be like between us? Having these inane discussions? Next thing you know, we'd be complaining about the weather.

"Anyway," Toby said. "Milo is going to stay in the Shack. That okay, babe?"

"If he doesn't mind lizards," I said and smiled at him. But then I looked away quickly. I couldn't get over how hot he was. He was so hot, he was smoking.

"Lizards?" Milo asked.

"Oh, yeah, we have these horrible little lizards in there," Toby said. "But I had it fumigated last week, so they might have scurried."

"I don't mind," Milo said. "I just appreciate you two letting me crash there until I find a place."

"No problem, buddy," Toby said and gave him a good-natured slap in the back. "I've been wanting you out here for years. Now you're here. It's gonna be awesome!"

Awesome wouldn't begin to describe what I wanted it to be. If only Milo would look me in the eye. And I wasn't dating Toby.

"Yeah, awesome," Milo said and glanced at me, then away quickly.

"Well, Holly," Toby said and chuckled, then gave me a quick peck on the cheek. "It looks like it's you, me and him. Think you can handle that?"

To be honest, I didn't know if I could.

○8

Over the next few weeks, Milo settled into the little guest house, the one we'd affectionately dubbed the Shack, at the back of our house. It was small but had its own bath. Toby had once used it as a makeshift studio when he first started producing, but as his business got bigger, he outgrew it and began renting a larger space. But the Shack had a nice bed, a cool couch and a flat-screen TV. And being minutes from the beach didn't make it suck, either.

I rarely saw Milo as Toby had him out meeting people and booking gigs. They'd come home really late, later than me and I didn't get home from my gigs until after two or so in the morning. We were like ships passing in the night. Oh, we still knew each other was there. We just didn't make a fuss about it.

Milo would come from the Shack into the house to get the occasional milk or beer. Sometimes he'd dine with Tony and me. Sometimes he'd come in to get Toby so they could go surf or whatever. We'd chat in passing, asking each other how it was going. He'd ask me about how I got to California. I told him I'd come out here to be a singer but fell in love with DJing. We had nice, pleasant conversations, yet neither of us dared overstep our boundaries. He was just a guy staying with his best friend until he found his own place. I was just the good girlfriend who allowed that.

So, he and I didn't connect. We kept our distance. We made it a point to stay away from each other. What else could we have done? I wasn't about to fuck up my relationship with my awesome boyfriend for a fling and that's what Milo would have been. And he wasn't about to upset his best friend by sleeping with his girl. Why should he have? Any lust or feelings we might have had were pushed aside. We knew we both had it good with Toby and neither one of us wanted to rock the boat.

That didn't keep me from fantasizing about rocking that boat, though. And those fantasies would come out full bore when I was having sex with my boyfriend. We got really loud and I sometimes thought about Milo hearing us and wondering how it made him feel. Jealous? Turned on? Maybe a little of both? But just thinking about him made the lust in me come out and if that meant I had to fuck my boyfriend's brains out, then so be it. I just couldn't contain it.

However, as hard as we fought it, something was bound to happen. It had to come to a head. Milo and I had too much sexual tension for it not to.

It happened on the day the air conditioning went out and the repairman couldn't make it until the next. I was so hot, I had stripped down to my panties and bra and was doing chores around the house. I didn't mind doing chores for our little beach house. It was the perfect home that we'd made ours. I loved its exposed wooden beams and the old wood floor and the curved archways. We'd made it cool and hip with flea market finds like the nearly worn out Persian rug in front of the midcentury modern soda and the chunky wood credenza that held our big flat screen TV. The art on the walls was eclectic and ranged from prints of famous works to local artists who sold their work along the beach. It was home and I felt so good here. I loved that it belonged to us, to Toby and I, and we'd made this home together. It suited us to a "T." That's why I didn't mind cleaning it. I'd take my time and dust and vacuum and put things away. Because the house wasn't that big, it didn't take much time to keep it tidy.

After I was done, I remembered that I'd just downloaded some new tunes, so I grabbed my MP3 player, sat down on the couch and put in my ear buds. Using the ear buds rather than the sound dock allowed me to get closer to the music and escape into it. It was just me and the music and there was no other place I'd rather be.

I soon became enraptured in the music sitting on the couch. I was also getting very hot. Without the air conditioner, the house was really heating up. So, I got down on the cool floor and lay there, my feet flat on the floor and my knees in the air, enjoying the music playing in my ear. I smiled because this was the reason I loved DJing—music. There was something about a good song, a good beat, that made me feel so alive and invigorated. Being a DJ meant I could share that with others.

I don't know how long I had lain there when I saw Milo's feet walking across the floor and into the adjacent kitchen. Toby was at work and he was practicing in the Shack. My heart began to race. I knew he was just there to get some cereal or whatever, but having him there alone with me while I was in my skivvies was a little unnerving. What should I do? Get up and race into the bedroom and throw something on? Or… Maybe I should do nothing.

Nothing sounded like a good option but then I thought about Toby. I should get up and pretend to be embarrassed or something. But I didn't move. Something made me hold out to see what Milo *might* do. I knew it wasn't right, but I wanted to at least see if he was as interested in me as I was in him. I had it bad for him and I knew I should have just let well enough alone but sometimes… Well, sometimes a girl just doesn't use good common sense when it comes to these things.

So I just lay there and pretended not to notice him. I felt his eyes on me from across the room, as if he was ascertaining what, exactly, this situation was. Or, possibly, could be. I liked the way he intently held his gaze on me. I liked the fact that I knew he liked what he saw, just like he liked what he saw the other day at the beach when I'd been in my chocolate brown bikini, the one that was a little small on top so that my boobs popped out a little and gave me great cleavage. I'd caught him staring at me several times, at my cleavage. I knew he was looking at me, at my body, and thinking about what he was missing out on. All men do that. They always have and they always will. The grass might not actually be greener on the other side, but it certainly looks prettier.

I felt that way from time to time, too. Especially right about now. The grass was looking mighty fine!

Milo moved in a little closer. My heart beat even more rapidly, if that was possible. Now. Now was the time. But did I have the nerve? What was I trying to prove? This couldn't go anywhere. But, somehow, I found myself wanting to do this, wanting to tease him a tiny bit, to show him a little of what I had. I parted my legs a little and slid my hand down my flat stomach and to the top of my panties. I was just about to put my hand into them when he spoke.

"I know you know I'm here," he said. "Don't do that in front of me."

But I couldn't stop. No, I *wouldn't* stop. He had to see this; he had to see me pleasuring myself. I wanted him to see it. It wasn't right and I shouldn't have been doing it, but I wanted to so badly. I ignored him, and my hand slipped into my panties and went down and down until it was resting on the place where his eyes were. He could see the wet spot on them, on the panties. He could see my need for him.

He walked out.

Oh, *fuck.* Oh, no. What had I done? I took off the ear buds and threw them to the side, feeling the sting of embarrassment on my cheeks, heating up my body. Would he tell Toby? Fuck! I was up the creek and there wasn't a damned paddle in sight. I was about to sit up when I heard something. His footsteps. What the hell? I froze.

Our eyes locked as Milo came back in. Without a word he headed for me, towards me. He bent down to his knees and pulled my legs apart, slipping his body in between them. I started aching for his touch. *Touch me, touch me, touch me. Touch me now; touch me everywhere and all at once. Let me feel you touching me. Kiss me a little while you're at it.*

But he wasn't that easy.

"Want me?" he breathed.

I moaned and nodded at him, sitting up to meet him. I could feel his body heat. He was hot, literally, quite hot for me. That made me even more turned on.

"Want me?" he asked again, this time more loudly. "Tell me you want me."

"I want you," I moaned and longed to pull him in close to me.

He stared into my eyes, still not moving. Then he gently grabbed the side of my bra and pulled it back a little as if to get a better look at my breast. His finger slipped in and grazed my nipple. Ummm… Oh, fuck, fuck, fuck! I wanted to scream at him to suck on my nipple, on both of them, to devour my breasts and my body and me. But I didn't move. I sat there and allowed him to play with me, to toy with me. To do whatever he wanted to do.

His other hand was pushing the other cup of my bra back and he stared at my breast, just stared. It seemed to take forever for him to push it down and then reach in with his mouth and suck my nipple in.

I moaned with pleasure and arched my back. I started to grab his head and kiss him but he gave me a look that told me to sit still. So I did. I sat still as he ate at my breasts, taking turns with each one to pleasure me. His hands were scooping them up and pushing under the bra and squeezing them tightly.

He slipped his arm around my back and unsnapped my bra, setting my breasts free. There were there, in front of him, hanging softly and waiting for more. I thrust my chest out at him, inviting him in to do even more than he was already doing and he took his cue, bent down and gave me more sucking, more nibbling and a little biting. It was too much. I could have come just from that, just from him playing with my breasts, taking his time to really arouse me while he had his fun.

Soon my pussy began to ache for a little attention. I sat up taller and spread my legs out wider. He settled in and I began to move my crotch against his shirt then right at his belt, then on his belt buckle. I liked the coolness of it grazing my clit, backwards and forwards and backwards and forwards. A simple yet so effective motion.

He was hard. He was so hard. I could see the outline of his erect and quite yummy looking cock through his pants. I wanted to pull it out and suck on it, suck every bit of juice that was trapped in there wanting release. I moved my crotch down until it was against his dick and there I moved against it, feeling its hardness and it girth and length. He was packing, that was for sure. I could only imagine how good that thing would feel once it was inside of me, which, hopefully, would be soon. I'd have it. I'd have it *all.*

I was caught up in the moment. Nothing could have stopped me. Nothing could have gotten in my way. Nothing stood between me and his cock. *Nothing.*

That is, nothing but Toby taking an early day.

Milo was still sucking at my breasts when I looked over his shoulder to see Toby. I was so startled I couldn't do anything. I didn't even gasp. I think my eyes might have popped out of my head, but then I noticed something odd. He wasn't moving. He was just watching us doing the dirty little things we were doing. He appeared enthralled, in awe. It was odd. It was like he… Well, it was like he didn't mind. I could tell he was aroused, too. His dick was getting hard and pressing against the worn-out khakis he'd had forever and refused to get rid of. I stared at his dick for a moment, thinking about how big and stiff it looked right then and my mind wandered to another scenario, where he wanted me like this in front of him, as if I were his favorite porn star or something. Did he imagine me doing it with another man? If so, what did he think about what we were doing right now in front of him? But I was probably just trying to figure out a way to make this okay. But was I imagining that? Was I imagining his arousal? His dick didn't lie, that was for sure. Did I want to have sex with Milo so badly that I finding any excuse I could to go through with it? Maybe.

But Toby… What was he doing? He just stood there and acted like… Well, like there was nothing wrong with what

Milo and I were doing. He and I locked eyes and he nodded, as if he knew I would do this all along, as if he knew it would someday come down to this. And it had.

As we stared at each other, I realized that this was embarrassing, *too* embarrassing. I was just so ashamed of myself, of my lust, I couldn't stand it. Could the floor please just swallow me up now? Please?

"We're not fucking!" I exclaimed and pounded on Milo's back. "Stop! Stop, Milo!"

He glanced over to see Toby and his mouth dropped. He started to move away, but Toby threw up his hand and halted him.

"We're not fucking!" I said again. "We're not fucking!"

"I heard you the first time," Toby said and smiled slightly, shaking his head.

What. The. Fuck?

He leaned against the wall and said, "Keep going."

Milo and I glanced at each other, then back at him. Was this a trick?

"Toby, listen, I—" I started but he stopped me.

"Just do it," he said and nodded at me. "It's fine with me."

"But we're not fucking," I told hm.

"No, you're not," he said. "Not yet anyway. You can though, if you like."

My mouth dropped a little. Milo looked like he was seeing things. I didn't know what to do. Toby did.

"I get it," Toby said. "I knew this would happen one day. It's cool."

Wow. Really? Had he just said that? Seriously? Was he serious? What was he doing? Right now, he was moving over towards us.

Milo stared at him, disbelieving. He started to say something but Toby shook his head and leaned down and kissed me hard. I hesitated at first then returned the kiss, licking at his lips and wanting his hands all over me.

Toby pulled back and said, "Your turn, Milo."

My mouth dropped to the floor. *Your turn Milo?* Was he serious? That was, like, totally cool with me! But I still had a hard time believing he was okay with all of this.

"Go ahead," he said and jerked his head a little at me.

Milo just stared at him.

"Go for it," he said with nonchalance.

Wait. Was I hearing this right? Was he the coolest boyfriend in the world or what? Or was this a trick, a ploy? What was it, exactly?

"I don't know if I can do this," Milo said.

"No, you can," he said. "Fuck her. And then I'll fuck her. I mean, if that's okay with you, Holly."

He stared at me. He wasn't pissed off or anything. Then I got it, I understood. Some guys weren't threatened like that. They were okay with sharing and with joining in. Toby was one of those guys. I could live with that. Toby was, like, sexually liberated or something. And that made me want to be sexually liberated. I might just be in for the fuck of my life. Knowing that made me feel embolden. It made me so hot I couldn't stand it. Well, then, let's get the show on the road.

I felt Milo's hesitation. I was a little hesitant, too. I was still slightly in shock but not so much so that I wasn't willing to take action. You only live once, right? I got to it and I got to it by taking control of the situation.

"You want me to fuck him?" I asked Toby.

"No," he said. "I want you to fuck both of us."

I smiled at him and said, "I'm gonna fuck him and you're gonna watch. I am going to suck every bit of cum out of him into my pussy. And then I'm going to do it to you."

My dirty talk pleased Toby to no end. A deep smile came across his face and he nodded at me. We were on the same wavelength. I knew I loved him for a reason.

But what about Milo? He sat there, looking slightly stunned, yet oddly pleased. He liked this idea, too. He was into it. It was a fantasy for guys, too, right? I knew then and there we were all three in for a really fun afternoon. That pleased me to no end. And I was ready to get this thing started.

I turned to Milo. "You ready for me?"

He nodded. "I am."

Good answer. I grinned at him and then I went for it. I went for it with gusto, with everything I had. I was so turned on, I think I might have went for it even if Toby hadn't wanted it. There was no stopping me now. I was a woman on a mission.

I grabbed Milo by the jawbone and pulled his face to mine. Our lips crushed into each other's and we moaned loudly as our tongues touched. I pressed my naked chest into his, loving the feeling of Toby's eyes on me as I did so, as I pushed my tits into his hard chest. It felt so good to have my naked tits squeezed almost flat against him.

"Watch me, baby," I said to Toby. "Don't take your eyes off me."

He was sitting to the side now, watching us like we were live-action porn or something. He nodded. He was into it. That was so cool it made me smile. I turned back to Milo and kissed him again, this time harder, thrusting my tongue onto his mouth so he could suck on it, then he gave me his and I sucked on it, drawing circles with my tongue on his. We were eating at each other, devouring each other as my boyfriend watched. It was so hedonistic, so downright dirty, I could have come just from the thought of it.

I started to undress him, wanting him naked, wanting him in me. His shirt came off, then his pants and boxers and then he was naked, lying on top me, me still in my soaking wet panties. His hand was between my legs, stroking me there, stroking my pussy, which began to ache like it had never ached before. I had to have his mouth there first, before his cock, his lips nibbling at my lips, down there, eating at me, sucking at me. So, I pushed him down and his mouth found my naked flesh and it welcomed him as my legs opened wide so he could do his work.

A finger slipped into my panties and touched the soft skin there, which was swollen with longing, with lust. Then the finger tugged at the panties and they were off, cast aside and I was totally naked in front of these two men whose eyes were all over my just waxed and smooth pussy. I felt so strong then, so womanly, so powerful. That's what they wanted, what I had between my legs. The looks on their faces told me as much.

I opened my legs wider and gave them a better look, wanting them to look, wanting them to want it, my pussy, and to want me, this woman who was offering herself for one afternoon of pure, unadulterated pleasure. *Come on, gentlemen, don't disappoint.*

They didn't.

Milo traced one finger down my slit, just like that, just so softly, before he stuck it in and moved it around a little. I writhed as he did that, moved against this finger and moaned in ecstasy. I was so wet, I was dripping.

"Suck me," I told him. "Suck my pussy."

His head went between my legs and his lips grazed my lips just ever so slightly. I shuddered with lust, wanting more. He gave it to me. He began to eat at me, sucking at me, stroking me with his tongue. I sat there and began to grind against his face a little, looking up at Toby who was watching with rapt attention. Without a word he got up and nudged Milo aside and scooped up my legs, pulling them off the floor a little and he dove in, sucking me and licking me with a flat, solid tongue, doing what he always did to me, making me come. And I came loudly, throwing my head back as a deep roar came out of me, and I began to grind until it was done.

Oh, yeah. That felt too damned good. I was just catching my breath when Toby gave me a long, hard kiss then moved aside. I stared at him, then back at Milo. It was time.

"Fuck me now," I told Milo.

He didn't hesitate. He was too turned on to wait much longer. He turned me over and I got up on all fours. Even though it was only a few seconds, it seemed to take forever for him to stick his hard cock in. I was dying for it. Then he did it. He stuck it in and we moaned in unison as we were joined together. He grabbed my ass and began to pound into me, holding my ass tight and hard as he fucked me dirty like that.

I held on for the ride but I wanted more. I stared at Toby and licked my lips. That was his cue. He came over to me and unzipped his pants and pulled his hard cock out. Then it was in my mouth and I was sucking it as I got fucked from behind. It was almost too much. I wanted to come and I wanted to get fucked and I wanted to suck Toby's hot semen out of him. All at once.

Just then Milo gave me a hard slap across the ass. I shuddered. Now it *was* getting dirty. More, more, please. He gave me another and rubbed the spot, then reached around and grabbed my tit, squeezing it, before slipping his hand between my legs and then finding and rubbing my clit. He did that for a moment, then moved his hand. What was he doing? I didn't know but I was overjoyed and really happy when his finger made its way down between my cheeks and then into my ass. Oh, yes! He slipped his finger in as he fucked me and I almost howled with pleasure. I wanted more, more, more! Give it to me! It was too much!

He kept it up until I was nearly exhausted. I wanted to finish Toby off but he stopped me, shaking his head and then bent to kiss me as Milo fucked me. He thrust his tongue in so I could suck on it as I was getting fucked from behind, with a finger in my ass. And then I came. I came so hard I almost bit into Toby's tongue. He moved just in time, squeezing a breast as the orgasm exploded inside of me. And then Milo came, came hard, pumping into me so much I thought he might break me.

But it wasn't over. Not just yet. Now it was Toby's turn.

He grabbed me up under the arms and pulled me to him, crushing his lips against mine. He walked me over to the wall and pushed me up against it. My legs opened wide and he got between them, pushing his hard cock into me, wanting me, feeling me, devouring me. Milo came over to us and moved my hair back from my neck, then slid his tongue down it, sucking at it as Toby fucked me. I turned my head to his and we kissed hard. His hand went to a breast and he grabbed it, squeezed it then bent to suck a nipple into his mouth. Toby grabbed the other one and tweaked it as Milo ate at my other. I loved that. It felt so good. I loved the feeling of my boyfriends dick inside me as his best friend's mouth was on my tit, sucking at it, owning it, making it his. But I wasn't his. I was Toby's. But then again, I realized, I was neither of theirs. I was mine. I belonged to me. I was getting more out of this than I could have ever imagined.

Milo's hand was now on his dick stroking it as Toby fucked me. We slid down the wall and then onto the floor and Toby got to it, fucking me. I fucked back and Milo got beside us and kissed me hard. I kissed back then concentrating on Toby, staring into his gorgeous eyes, loving him and loving that he'd given me this gift of a ménage à trois. I wanted to tell him that, to thank him and make him promise we'd do it again but I was too busy. I was too focused on fucking him. He was coming and he was coming harder than I'd ever seen him come, pumping into me like a mad man, like a man on mission and that mission was to give me all he had. And so he did, coming hard and I was so turned on, I came too, for the third time that day.

When it was over, Toby rolled off me and Milo lay down on the other side. We all lay on the floor, sweating, feeling just a little air from the overhead fan as we got our breaths back. I turned on my side and slide between them, between my two men, getting their manly sweat all over me. Milo got up close to me from behind and Toby stayed in front. We lay like that for a little while and I moved between them, feeling their masculinity and allowing them to feel me, my femininity. I loved feeling their hard chests and big arms and muscles and bodies while I was squeezed in between them. I loved knowing that their large, semi-hard cocks would soon be ready to fill me again. It was almost too much to take in.

It would be a little bit before Toby was ready again but I could feel Milo's cock stiffening as he slipped it between my ass cheeks. I loved the feeling of him trying to get in. I wanted it again. I was ready. I was so turned on I didn't know if I'd ever be turned off again. He opened my legs a little and pressed his dick against my pussy which was already waiting for it. He slipped it in and I kissed Toby, softly and fully, licking his lips, opening my mouth up wide to suck them in a little, then slipping my tongue into his mouth as Milo fucked me, fucked my pussy from behind. *Yes, fuck me, fuck my pussy as I kiss my boyfriend.*

Toby slipped his hand between my legs and laid it flat, moving his fingers just slightly so I could move against it and get my groove on. Milo fucked me slowly, gently, as Toby bent to kiss my breasts softly, to touch them gently, to cup them and to kiss them. I just lay there and enjoyed it, enjoyed the feeling of being with these two in this way. The sensations were sensual, so soft and even a little sweet. We were sweaty and slid against each other. It was raw and hot and felt so hedonistic. It felt right, as if we should always be doing this. If I was lucky, we would.

I ran my hand in Toby's hair then slid it down his chest and then to his cock. He was now hard again. Once more. He was ready. I took hold of it and began to fondle it as Milo kept fucking me slowly from behind. I rubbed it with just a little pressure, wanting his cum to squirt into my hand. Milo kept at it, too, filling my pussy with his dick as I stroked Toby's cock with my hand, as he rubbed my clit with his finger. Ummm… There it was. I felt it wash all over me, the orgasm, and literally take me over. Milo was coming inside of me again, giving a slight, soft moan and I felt Toby's dick move and then his cum shoot out into my hand as I came.

Toby's eyes opened just as mine did and we stared into each other's eyes. We didn't ask what this meant. It was just too good for words. We'd both enjoyed it, maybe for different reasons, but we'd had so much fun. And Milo? How did he feel? He was hugging my waist just then, letting me know he felt pretty damn good.

Without saying a thing, I held my hand up to my mouth and licked Toby's cum off, swallowing it. His eyes widened. He'd never seen me do anything like that. I licked it until it was gone. He grabbed the back of my head and pulled me to him, kissing me hard. We kissed for a long few seconds, then he pulled back.

We didn't say a word. What was there to say? Well, I had a suggestion: Could we do it again? And how soon? But did I dare say it? Did I dare ask for more when I'd been given so much? No, not just yet. But after they'd both fully recovered? Yes, I'd ask for it again and again.

I turned onto my back and they did too. We lay on the floor and stared up at the ceiling. It was over now. But, no, I liked to think it had only just begun.

Merci

CONTENTS—MERCI

Man on a Mission

I didn't even want to come to Paris. But as I stared at him, ready to devour me, I knew I'd made the right decision, even though sometimes he drove me absolutely insane.

"I know what your problem is," I said to him once.

"And what's that?" he asked.

"You don't believe in love."

"Oh, I believe in love," he replied. "I'm just not fooled by it."

He said that to me just shortly after we met. He believed in love; he just wasn't fooled by it. I was. I was fooled by love. I was fooled by him.

He was always a bit of a smartass. But then again, so was I. His name was François and he liked smoking, drinking cognac and taking long walks in the park. He was everything I'd ever wanted in a man and nothing I needed. He was alive with lust for me. I couldn't take my eyes off him. I wanted to, but I just couldn't. He was handsome, French and had a cool confidence that came across as cocky and arrogant. That's the part of him I had to get over in order to get to this. First impressions are never good but I'd given him a second chance to change my mind about him. And he had. Now he had me eating out of the palm of his hand. His cocky confidence had paid off.

He licked his lips and stared at me. I liked the way he licked his lips; I liked the way he stared. He was going to give it to me good and I couldn't wait. We were done with the formalities. It was time to get down to business.

He didn't hesitate. He came at me full throttle, a man on a mission. He didn't take his eyes off of me as he approached. He couldn't have. It was all about me; me being conquered by him. I wouldn't have it any other way.

And then, there he was. Right in front of me. He didn't hesitate to turn me around or push me up against the wall so that my back was to him. He went for it and took it. It was going to be rough this time. I liked it rough. He liked to give it to me rough.

A grunt came out of my mouth as he grabbed my ass. Delight filled my body as he began to play with me, as his hand slid between my ass cheeks.

"Already wet, aren't you?" he asked hotly.

I nodded as he continued, as his hands played with me. I widened my stance and he bent behind me, pushing his face into my pussy. His face was between my legs and he was eating me, eating every square inch of my pussy, licking and slurping and really getting into it. He moaned a little and pulled back to finger me.

I moaned and began to ride his face until I felt it. The orgasm was right there. It was intense and so ready to explode in my body. It did just that as he sucked at me. I kept coming and coming. Once it had abated, he turned me around, gave me one quick, deep kiss then bent me over the hall table, pushing me face-down on it.

"Oh, God," I moaned. "Yes! Do it, do it, do it!"

He did it. I heard his zipper and then felt his cock against my ass. That's when I began to shiver even more. I wanted it so *bad*. As soon as he thrust his hard cock into me, I clawed at the table. He reached around and grabbed at my breasts. I rose up and grabbed the back of his head, pulling his mouth to mine. We licked and sucked at each other's mouths as he fucked me. He gave me a hard thrust that sent my head back down. A long moan came out of my mouth. He was totally in control of me. I loved it.

Now, he was fucking me, concentrating on fucking me.

He turned me around and put me up on the table. My legs opened wide and invited him in. He hesitated, staring at me, at my pussy, which wanted him back in. I wasn't in the mood for games, so I grabbed his shirt and pulled it over his head, then leaned in and kissed his chest and nipples, licking my way up to his neck, which I sucked and kissed. I clawed at him with my hands until he grabbed them and put them on his cock and together we stroked it.

I stared down at it, so hard it trembled a little. Then I got up off the table and bent before him and took it in my mouth. I wanted to give him a little of what he'd given me, but just to the point he could no longer take it. That didn't take long. I gave good head and before I was ready to stop he grabbed me and pulled me back up to him, giving me a hot, hard kiss before pushing me back onto the table.

Oh, yes. It was time to get the show on the road. Now, it was time for him to really fuck my brains out. I'd never get enough, even after I left for the day. I'd think of him until we met again, tomorrow.

He was in; his cock was in me, fucking me. *It felt so good.* I grabbed onto his shoulders and stared into his dark eyes. They were beautiful eyes and they told me everything he'd never dare say. They told me he loved doing this to me and that he loved me. I knew it already. It was just nice to have confirmation.

I started to fuck him back. He bent over and pressed his face into my neck, which he sucked and licked and stroked with his tongue. It was almost too much. I was almost right there, right at orgasm. But before I could come, he started driving it in even more, even harder and that made me want to play more, to get more, to have more of this feeling, of this intense sexual pure joy feeling.

Every single inch of his hard cock filled me. It was difficult to contain the excitement and before he could give another thrust, the orgasm just jumped on me and rode me hard, just like he was riding me—good, hard, steady but fast. I exploded with passion. *I could not get enough.* I was coming so hard and so good I was shaking. He was shaking me to the core, just like he always did.

He was coming, too. He was coming just like I was coming and there was nothing either of us could do but hold onto it and beg it to last. It was over sooner than we both liked and we were kissing, hugging, holding onto each other after it was gone.

We were panting and then he was pulling away from me. We stared into each other's eyes unblinkingly, uninhibited but didn't say a word. There was nothing to say.

It's true. Paris is for lovers.

An American in Paris

"Nina," he would call to me as if from another room, from inside a dream. "Come here. Come now."

Come here. Come now. I would go to him without hesitation.

I was only thirty-one then. Thirty-one. Thirty. One. Not young but certainly not old. More impressionable than I'd ever admit. I could have been nineteen—I was that sexually innocent. Or repressed. I like to think of it as innocence. But it wasn't. It was repression. All of it. I repressed myself. I was a good girl and good girls don't like bad sex. At least not until they have some.

I liked it. No, I loved it. I loved when he took charge and pushed me up against the wall. I loved being taken all over the room—on the couch, on the table, on the floor. I loved how our love making wasn't resigned to just one place. I loved looking into his fierce eyes as we fucked ourselves silly. I loved our games of dominance and submission.

But sex wasn't that big of deal to me. Sure, I'd had it but it didn't really move me. I didn't fantasize about it. It was what it was. To be honest, he didn't do it for me at first. No man really did. I just wasn't that interested in sex. Sure, I had had good sex—sometimes even great sex—and all that, but it wasn't something I craved. It was more like a diversion.

But that was all about to change.

I once told a friend, "Men love women and women love vibrators." And that's where I got most of my love from, from a plastic, battery-powered device. It felt good, but there was always something missing. Vibrators don't have hands and lips and they don't have emotions. He had emotions, by the truckload.

He. Him. François. French. Handsome, aloof, a bit of an asshole when he wanted to be and sometimes when he was just being himself. I didn't appreciate him, didn't appreciate what he was doing to me, how he was making me feel. And he made me feel things I never imagined. Things... They were just feelings. No.

No. No. No.

François. François standing in the rain at the entrance to the metro station waiting for me. François laughing wildly at a bad joke somewhere in the middle of Paris. François. French sex god. Young François. Older than me by only three years. François who made me so horny I would do nothing but fantasize about us fucking in the bathtub, in the alley, in his big bed.

François didn't show me much of Paris. No, we mostly stayed indoors which was much more fun and exciting than the streets of Paris could ever be to me.

I wasn't even supposed to go to Paris. My roommate, James, talked me into it and I went partly because I could and partly because I should. It was a once in a lifetime thing, an opportunity to live abroad. To be free. To let go of all responsibility.

James had managed to pull off some major European sales coup and his company wanted to transfer him to their branch in France so he could babysit the details. I was only living with him until I could find a place of my own. I didn't have a place to live due to selling the house after our divorce. We'd miraculously come out ahead on the house and actually had money to split. In addition to that, I had a healthy savings account due to the fact that my mother had always taught me to save money on my own because, "You never know what might happen." She had been right. I hadn't envisioned the divorce but once it was done, I was in a good financial position to do something like this. So, why not?

I went to Paris out of boredom, out of desperation. I was young, impressionable. I went because I was underemployed. My job, while financially rewarding, just bored me to tears. It was the same hum-drum day after day. I didn't have anything to lose by going. I could find another job, but an opportunity like this? That was a once in a lifetime thing. In fact, if I didn't go, I would be losing out.

Life, simply, wasn't all that exciting for me during that time. I'd done everything right, just like those cheap little life lessons that movies and books are so found of giving us. Work hard, get rewarded. What a crock of shit. I had worked hard on my marriage just to see him walk out the door. I was bitter about that, too.

"For maybe a year," James said and smiled, the tiny laugh lines that surrounded his beautiful blue eyes crinkling a little. "It'll be fun living in a new place with someone I already know." He smiled again, then winked at me, adding, "And love."

He was so happy. I stared at him, starting to get convinced. He had an infectious happy air about him. He was always smiling, giving compliments, living life the way it should be lived. He was tall, handsome and gay. If only he'd been straight, I'd been a happy, happy girl. But he wasn't. Even so, he was my best friend and treated me like a princess. He was better to me than my ex-husband had ever been.

"It'll be great, Nina," he said and smiled and smiled.

I wasn't so sure. I'd been to Paris as a tourist and found the Parisian people to be... Well, to be...*French*. Very much so.

I almost told him to go without me. I had my own little job and my own little life. And here he wanted me to drop everything and leave. He told he needed me to go with him, that he didn't want to be all alone in a city like that. He said we could have so much fun and that if I did, he'd make it up to me.

"They're going to rent me an apartment," he said and smiled again, this time more widely. "And a car."

He was so damn proud of himself. I looked away from him, finding excuses not to go. Okay. Here was one: The thought of driving in Paris gave me hives. What if I got caught in that roundabout or whatever it was called at the Arc de Triomphe and couldn't get out of it?

Was that it? Was *that* the only excuse I could find not to go to Paris? I mulled it over in my mind. Should I go? Should I stay? I weighed the options, the pros and the cons. There just wasn't that much for me in Atlanta at the time. And the fact was I could take a taxi or the Metro wherever I wanted in the city. I didn't *have* to drive if I didn't want to. That was a pro. The other pro? I hated my job and I was sick of Atlanta and my friends were busy with their own lives.

And while I could date, I hated the thought of seeing my ex-husband out. What if I ran into him with some new woman? Could I handle that? I didn't know if I could. I knew he was moving on, seeing other people, dating. I was doing none of those things. I was stuck, not knowing what move to make next. Paris, at that time, seemed like the only viable option to get my life up and running again. It would jerk me out of my slight depression and dissipate the bitterness a little.

So, what was the con about going? Oh, driving around the city. Oh, and the French people being a little... *French*. Hmmm...

"Nina," James said, smiling slightly. "How about it? Want to go or not?"

"Sounds great," I said and smiled back at him. "When do we leave?"

CB

The first month was hell.

I was alone most of the time because James was busy being important. He was constantly working. I didn't know anyone. I didn't do anything. I just sat in our nice but old Parisian apartment with the high ceilings and beautiful crown moldings and rooms that were modernized and large. The wood floors were well-worn and a spectacular herringbone. The furniture was comfortable but modern. It was an apartment people only dream of having in Paris. I'd sit on the couch, or even in the chair, and try to find something on TV, which wasn't an easy task because I didn't learn the French language easily. Sure, I was soon picking up some here and there and could understand a little and even speak a little, but, mostly, I was lost. I don't know how many conversations I bumbled my way through. Good thing a lot of people in Paris actually spoke English.

I hated it. I wanted to go home. I told James as much over dinner.

"Go out and meet some people," he said.

"Who?" I asked, getting frustrated. "The doorman? The lady at the market? Who?!"

"Is it who or whom?" he asked and stared at the ceiling as if he were really trying to figure this one out. "I've been speaking so much French I think I'm beginning to question my English."

"Don't do this right now," I said.

"Do what?" he replied and stared back at me.

"Act like I'm an asshole and then act like an asshole yourself," I said. "I know I'm being an asshole, but I just don't like it here."

He stared numbly at me. I wanted to yell something at him. Exactly what I didn't know. Maybe I was jealous that he was acclimating better than me and would come home late in the evenings happy as a lark while I'd been sitting in that apartment doing nothing. It was too much. I felt too out of place, too much like a foreigner. My comfort level had been compromised and I didn't know if I'd ever feel at home here in the most beautiful city on earth. Maybe I was just a fool and couldn't see that life had handed me—on a silver platter, no less—an extraordinary gift. I couldn't see it, though, because I was very intimidated. And being intimidated made me angry.

The next day, James came home early. He called from the foyer, "I've got something for you!"

I didn't even move off the couch.

"Nina!" he hollered.

I ignored him, turned over and buried my face in the cushion.

I heard him mutter, "For God's sake," and then he rolled something into the living room.

"Nina?"

I ignored him.

He came over and pried me away from the couch and forced me to look at what he had bought me—a bicycle. One of those old European ones with a basket and a bell. It looked like a beach cruiser, the kind old women and men with DUI's ride. Oh, for God's sake.

"You've got to be kidding me," I said.

"It's great," he replied. "Don't you think? These bikes are really hip now."

I eyed it. "Did you find that in the garbage?"

"No!" he exclaimed. "I bought it."

"You *bought* it?"

"Yeah," he said. "Granted, it's second-hand but most people don't ride expensive bikes over here. Plus, it works." He demonstrated by ringing the bell. *Ding! Ding!*

The bike, even if it *were* hip, was old, slightly rusted and used to be some sort of electric blue color. The basket had seen better days. However, the lone flower that had survived was now a pale pink color, which didn't go with the electric blue at all. It was so ugly, it was bordering on hideous. If he thought I was riding that thing along the streets of Paris, he had lost his damned mind. I already felt like an out of place fool just walking around. Everyone else walked too; it wasn't that big of a deal. Nevertheless, *they* seemed to know where they were headed.

"Why don't people ride better bikes than this?" I asked.

"They'll get stolen."

I eyed the bike. Yeah. No one would want to steal that thing. I wouldn't even have to chain it up.

"Besides, with this one, you'll blend in more," he said, so damn proud of himself. "With the locals."

I just stared at him.

"Come on," he said and held out his hand. "Give it a try."

"No," I said. "I'm not riding that thing."

"Well, you said you wouldn't drive," he said. "This is a good option."

"No, it's not! I could get hit by a bus or a car or a rude Frenchman!"

"Come on," he said. "Give it a try."

"No," I snapped and started out of the room. "*You* give it a try, James."

"Nina, come on," he said, following me. "What do you have to lose?"

I sighed and told him I'd rather walk and that if I didn't start liking Paris soon, I'd be on the next plane out. I knew I was being a bitch, but I wasn't suited for a life abroad. I wasn't a cool expatriate. I was just me and being me right then didn't feel so good.

However, the next morning, the bicycle and I had a standoff. We stared at each other, each of us daring the other to do something. Well, I stared at it and it just looked like shit. But it won. It was either that or calling airlines looking for the best deal out of Paris. Why *not* give it a try? What *did* I have to lose? Not much. The bicycle won and I had to see what might be out there for me.

I rolled it out of the apartment, into the elevator and onto the street. I felt like a fool. I got on it and rode up the street, stopped at the corner and looked both ways, then I went another block, then two. Then I almost ran over some school children and pushed it back to the apartment.

The next day, I tried it again. And the day after that. Each day, I would go a little further and further until one day, I realized I had ridden around a great portion of the city. Well, at least all the touristy areas. I had been by the Louvre. I had been by the Eiffel Tower, down the Champs Elysees and over to Notre Dame. I'd even stopped by cafés and had lunch.

I felt pretty good about myself.

"See?" James said. "I told you you'd like it."

And I actually did. I was starting to enjoy Paris. It's a place that, while beautiful, one has to adapt to. It doesn't greet you and it doesn't open its arms. It's just there, daring you to like it—or not, it didn't care either way. And you have to like it, or even *love* it, because, well, it's Paris. And Paris doesn't give a damn what you think about it because it already knows how great it is. But I was beginning to like it even though, at first, it had intimidated the hell out of me. And I like to think that Paris was beginning to like me back. We were starting to get along just fine.

One of my favorite things to do was to watch couples from a park bench. I'd heard somewhere that the tourism board actually paid couples to come to the park and make out. It made the city seem more romantic. I didn't know if any of the couples I was watching had actually been paid—or if this was even true—but they really went at it. I'd watch them, but at the same time, I'd also feel a little like a voyeur. I wasn't that interested in doing it myself because of my divorce, but it did look like fun.

The French men were great, though a little off-putting. Like the city of Paris, they too intimidated me, but at the same time they shouldn't have. They would stare at me, somewhat smiling, like they knew all about me. I'd look away quickly and pray they wouldn't try to talk to me. They didn't. They didn't have to.

There seemed to be a discernible difference between American men and French men. With the French, there was no premeditation, no games to play. If they wanted you, it would only be a matter of time before they had you. There would be no issues to deal with. If they had a lover in the past that hurt them, once you showed up, she was gone from memory. It was all about you then, to them. There was more concentration. It was all about the one that in front of them at the time. When they kissed you, they kissed *you*. They gave it everything they had.

With American men, not so much. From my experiences, they were usually kissing you with one eye open so they could scout for other women they might like better. But maybe I was romanticizing French men. Maybe they did this too. Maybe *all* men did it.

But, in actuality, this was never a personal experience of mine, worrying about a man with a roaming eye. But I'd heard about it from girlfriends who had to play the game of love over and over until they finally pinned some bastard down to marry and procreate with. With me, I was the one looking around, trying to figure a way out. I hated commitment, even when I was married. I don't know why I hated it; maybe because once you seal that door off, it's hard to open back up.

Nevertheless, I would watch the French men and the French women coupling and eventually began to fantasize about that happening between me and a handsome man. My mind would hope for something like that to come along, though it did scare me a little, to be that open, that vulnerable. However, you can hope for something, you can wish, but if it's not meant to be yours, it won't ever come your way. And there's nothing you can do about it. I figured I was just going to be a spectator here and I would enjoy doing that. I was still hurt over my failed marriage and sometimes I just wished it would go away—the pain of loving someone and the pain of watching them leave your life, even though I had helped him walk out the door due to my commitment issues. But right then, I did long for a real man, someone who might suit me better. Someone I wouldn't want to push away.

The love I'd had was comfortable and nice. It was also monotonous. You get to know someone too well and you become too familiar with each other to ask for what you want. Sometimes you just get tired of pretending, of fantasizing; you want to play for real. Just because you do.

You don't have to explain everything. Not even to yourself. Why waste time on angst? That's what the couples in the park taught me. Sometimes, you just want to sit on a nice wool blanket and kiss the afternoon away. Being in love had made me forget about all the bad stuff, just as the couples were doing as they kissed. I wanted that back.

Maybe I was too uptight, too wound up. Maybe that would change someday but right then, I was fine with being like that. We are creatures of habit. From my experiences with the bicycle, I was learning that breaking habits came quite naturally to me. I was ready to kiss the sky and say goodbye to all that, to that former self that had held me back and held me down. I was just waiting on the right time and the right man. Luckily for me, neither made me wait very long.

Come Love Me Now

He was rich and he was bored. His name was François. I met him one day at a café while I had a croissant and a coffee.

I'd been reading an American newspaper and wondering what I could do with the rest of the day before I had to get back to the apartment. James wanted to invite some of his new work friends over and he wanted me there to meet them. The apartment also needed to be picked up and cleaned and then I had to do the shopping and then prepare the meal. Several years ago, I'd been a line cook in a really nice restaurant in Atlanta so I could whip something up in no time. But what would his French friends like? Would they respond to fried green tomatoes? I didn't think so, but you never know.

"Some of them are really good looking," he said. "I can't wait for you to meet them."

So, I had agreed. Now I was at a loss as to what to prepare.

"Bon jour."

I had been so lost in my thoughts I hadn't noticed when he'd approached me. And I was just about to take a sip of coffee when I heard his voice, which slightly startled me and made my hand shake, almost spilling the coffee. I set the cup down and looked up to see a tall man with a handsome face staring at me. I said, "Bonjour."

He began to speak French, speaking so fast I had a hard time picking up on any of the words. Normally, I could understand bits and pieces of sentences but with him I was at a loss.

I held my hand up. "I'm sorry. I don't speak French."

"Oh, American?" he said with his thick French accent, seemingly surprised.

"Yes," I said.

"Your face," he said and touched his face. "Very French looking."

I nodded. I was somewhat French looking. This had even happened to me in America, French people assuming I was also French. He wasn't the first person to come up to me and start speaking French. Just the other day, I'd had a mother and daughter, who were obviously from somewhere out in the boondocks, ask me directions to somewhere on the Metro. I had to explain to them as well that I was an American. They became angry because they didn't believe me and thought I was just making fun of them. People can be so weird.

"Oh," I said and nodded.

"Mind if I sit with you?" he asked. "All the other seats are taken."

I looked around at the crowded café and nodded. "Sure."

He smiled, sat down and lit a cigarette, then offered one to me. "Smoke?"

I shook my head. "No, thanks, I just had one." Unfortunately, I'd started back once I arrived in Paris. A lot of people smoked. I promised myself that I'd quit again soon.

He nodded and smiled a little. The waiter came up and he ordered, again in French, then the turned to me. "How long are you in Paris?"

"For about a year," I said.

"Oh, with your husband?" he asked and took a drag from the cigarette.

"No," I said. "With a friend. I'm not married. Anymore."

"Me either," he said, smiling. "Do you like the city?"

I nodded. "Very much so."

"Good, good," he said, then took the cup of coffee from the waiter, sipped it, sat it on the table and puffed on his cigarette. "What do you like best here?"

"Oh, I guess the museums," I said. "They're absolutely phenomenal. I got lost in the Louvre."

"Nice but too crowded," he said. "I like the Musée National d'Art Moderne. They have Matisse, Picasso, of course, Duchamp..."

He said it like a question, as if he didn't know if I'd ever heard of such artists. I nodded dumbly.

"I can take you sometime, give you a tour," he said. "You'd like it."

"Oh, no," I said quickly. "I wouldn't want to bother you."

"A beautiful woman never bothers a man," he said.

Beautiful woman? I almost blushed. *Almost.* I knew was pretty, but beautiful? It was nice to hear but my insecurity would never allow me to believe it. I did get looks from men and I knew I looked good. My hair was light brown and I usually pulled it into a high ponytail, which made me look younger than I was. My skin was slightly freckled, but not too much, and clear thanks to the simple beauty routine I'd started when I was younger. And I was never without my red lipstick, which made my full lips appear even fuller.

"What is your name?" he asked, cutting into my rambling thoughts.

"Nina," I said. "Yours?"

"François," he said and held out his hand. "Very nice to meet you."

I shook his hand and felt very nervous.

"Want to come?" he asked and took another drag of the cigarette. "I can take you today."

"Oh, no," I said and pointed at my bike. "I have to get back home soon. We're having a party tonight."

"But I thought you said you weren't married," he said.

"I'm not," I said quickly. "It's for my roommate, James." I stared at him. He was confused. "He's not my boyfriend or anything. He's gay. We're just… I don't how to explain it. He's working and I'm just visiting. He didn't want to come alone. I agreed to come with him, you know, to keep him company and stuff."

"Oh, that's nice," he said, nodding and putting his cigarette out. "I have a car, over there. We can drive."

He was being very pushy. I didn't like it. I glanced over at his car, a sleek black Mercedes sedan. *Nice*. But, no.

"Really, that's fine," I said. "I have to go."

He watched me stand up and nervously sort through my wallet for money to pay the tab. When I tried to set it down, he grabbed my hand and said, "I'll get it."

"Oh, that's okay."

"I insist."

I stared at him and nodded. "Thanks."

"Merci," he said.

"Excuse me?"

"Merci is what we say instead of 'thanks,'" he said, smiling. "So you say 'merci' in Paris. In French."

I knew that already. But the way he said it, the way it rolled off his tongue, gave me pause. It was like he was saying thank you to something else entirely.

"Oh, okay," I said, shaking myself slightly. "Then, merci."

"You're very welcome," he replied.

I nodded and started off, then felt bad. He wasn't a creep and I didn't have to jump up and run away like some backwoods idiot. I turned back around and said, "Would you like to walk to the museum with me?"

He grinned. And he grinned because he knew he had me. He jumped up and said, "Très bien. I would like that very much."

☙

François knew a lot about art and he knew how to make me feel comfortable. As we strolled the halls of the museum, I began to relax and wonder why I'd been so nervous before. So afraid.

That was the real problem, my cowardice. I was afraid to do anything outside my comfort level. This was because I didn't want to get hurt. I was afraid of giving myself over completely, to anything. François, however, didn't have this problem. He was not afraid to fully engage. He wasn't afraid to get overly involved.

"If you stop looking for reasoning, for a *reason* why the artist did what they did," he said and waved his hand at a Braque. "Then you can see it as just what the artist intended it to be. There is no reason to art. It's just art. Putting meaning into it is a waste of time. Americans always do that, instead of just enjoying the work."

My face flushed. I looked away from him quickly, then started walking quickly, wanting to get away from him. I hated the way everyone always had to make fun of Americans. It was just so typical. I got that a lot in Paris. It made me feel unwelcome and unwanted. I was sick of it, too.

"What's wrong?" he asked, catching up with me.

"Nothing," I said.

"Sorry, did I do something?" he asked and then started yammering away in French. I shook my head at him and he said, "Oh, I get it. You're American. I see."

You're American. I see. I saw, too. That didn't set well with me. I refrained from smacking the side of his smug face. Instead, I turned on my heel and made my way out.

He ran up behind me and grabbed my arm, stopping me. "I apologize, Nina."

I jerked my arm away and said, "You know what pisses me off? Everyone in the world wants Americans to respect their cultures but no one respects Americans."

He sighed heavily as if trying to understand me, then said, "That's not true."

"It's is," I replied. "And it's so hypocritical. America is a great place and we've done great things but everyone feels they have to criticize or make some sort of condescending comment about everything. Why?"

"No one is condescending," he said.

He was right. I was just feeling out of my element again. It was him making me feel this way. He was just so smug. Did he really think I cared what he thought? Well, I didn't. I didn't even know him.

"Sorry," he said. "I didn't realize that comment would upset you."

"Well, it did," I hissed and turned on my heel and headed out the door. Once I got outside, I looked up and down the street. Which way was the apartment? I always got so confused. But I didn't want to go to the apartment; I wanted to go home, to Atlanta. I wanted to go home so bad I ached. It wasn't lost on me that as soon as I started getting comfortable in Paris, something happened to screw it up. Maybe it was just my overwhelming insecurity.

I turned in the direction I thought was the right one and started to run. I felt like such a fool but couldn't help myself. I ran, then tripped and fell right on my face. I let out a cry and suddenly he was there, bent down, examining my face with concern.

"I'll take you home," he said, staring into my eyes. "And I'll help you."

"No," I said. "No, I—"

He ignored me and snapped his fingers and a man dressed in a black suit came up and helped him help me into his car, the black Mercedes I'd noticed earlier. What the hell? Then I realized someone else had driven his car to the museum. And it was this man, who just happened to be dressed in a chauffeur's uniform. Well, that made sense. François had a chauffeur. Not only was he handsome, he was unbelievably rich and knowing this made me feel like some stupid country bumpkin, though I was from one of the largest cities in America. I almost wanted to cry. I couldn't win. I could never, ever win. Why didn't I just give up and go home already?

"My bicycle," I said out of nowhere, almost panicking at the thought of leaving it. Why I was so concerned at that moment for it would be anyone's guess.

"I'll send Pierre back for it," he said.

So, that was the chauffer's name. After we were in the car, Pierre took the wheel and we were pulling away before I could blink. I almost panicked but then the side of my face throbbed. *Ouch*. It *hurt*.

I shouldn't have been surprised when the car drove out of the city limits and into the country then pulled up to a Château just outside Paris. It was breathtaking and so

French. It looked a little rundown, as if he hadn't bothered to keep it up. It was beautiful but it looked like was on its way down if someone didn't interfere. Yet, it was slightly decadent, something one might see in an old movie with subtitles.

He didn't seem to mind or even notice the way it looked, the slight decay. He just lived there, I could tell. It was just a house to him. To me, a foreigner, it was symbolic of all things French.

Inside looked about like the outside. The plaster on the ceiling was cracking and the once lovely wood floors were dull. The French provincial furniture was old and scratched and a little worn. Inside the huge living area was a small flat screen TV which looked totally out of place with the atmosphere and furniture and was much too small for the room. This made sense, though, because he didn't seem like a guy who watched a lot of TV. François excused himself and left me to marvel at the space.

"Are you rich?" I asked when he returned.

"My father was," he said, smiling. "But he never gave me anything but knowledge. Instead, I learned the business and made my own money. Now my father and I don't speak."

I stared at him.

"It might have something to do with my stepmother," he said and pressed an ice pack to my face. "But what does it matter?"

I guess it didn't. I looked around the room again, still not over the grandeur of the place. François watched me, noticing my awe.

"I inherited this from my grandfather," he said, waving his hand around the room.

Must be nice... My roots were firmly planted in a working class background. His, obviously, were planted somewhere else. We were so different. So, what was I doing here? I didn't know but I couldn't think of a reason to leave.

"Why did you divorce your husband?" he asked suddenly.

Did he just ask that? That made me a little uncomfortable, so I ignored him and looked away. I held the ice pack to my face, then went to a mirror to check myself. Phew! I had an ugly red scrape and a big bruise. How I'd fallen on my face like that was beyond me.

"Umm?" he asked

"Why did you divorce your wife?" I asked, turning around.

"Couldn't get along with her," he said. "She was little, how do you say… Hot-headed? A bit like you."

I wanted to smack him.

"So what happened to your husband?" he asked.

"Why are you so interested?" I shot back. If there's one thing that annoyed me was people who pried. I hated that.

"Did you cheat?" he asked, not letting it go.

"It's none of your business," I said. "But no, he cheated." However, I didn't confess, *I pretty much wanted him to*. I didn't say that I drove him away so that *I* could cheat, even though I never did. But I had wanted to. I wanted to feel the touch of another man, yet I never allowed myself that sort of freedom. I honored my vows not because of loyalty but because of default.

"Men are like that," he said, nodding, almost smiling.

"Is that what you did?"

He shrugged. "I had lovers when I was married but I don't count them as cheating."

"They didn't count?"

"No," he said. "They were just…flings. They meant nothing to me. My ex-wife, nonetheless, did cheat. She had a real lover, someone she loved very much. Which was fine. I no longer loved her."

"Why not?"

"I realized that she wasn't my type," he said.

His type? So that was the problem? Had that been my problem, my ex just wasn't my type? Did I have a type? I didn't know, but he was striking a cord, like he knew all about me and where I wanted to go. He was also insinuating that he could take me there. But I didn't know if I could handle going, so I turned on him, pushing him away and putting him in his place. It was a bitch thing to do but the thought of letting anyone close to me, even though I craved it, scared the hell out of me.

"You know something, François?" I said. "You're an asshole."

"Is that the name for it?" he asked. "I always wondered."

I rolled my eyes.

"Why don't you like me, Nina?" he asked softly.

"I don't know," I said. "But I just don't."

"You will someday," he said.

"No, I won't."

He nodded. "Yes, you will. You will like me very much. We will be lovers."

"I don't think so."

"Do you know they say that French men are the best lovers in the world?" he asked.

"Who's 'they'?" I asked. "Other French men?"

He threw his head back and laughed. "Good one. But no, women say it. And they're right."

"I'd never let you touch me," I said and put the ice pack down.

"Oh, yes, you will."

"No, I won't," I said.

"Oh, you'll be begging for it."

I paused, thinking I should be taken aback, but something in me wouldn't allow that. He was so cocky, so self-assured. Right then, I couldn't play the naïve card. I had to set him straight and put him in his place. So, I said, "Bullshit."

"It's true," he said. "But you're different, difficult, a challenge. I like that."

I didn't feel different. I didn't like it much, either. I wanted to be that sexy, sexual creature. I wanted to be that open but I couldn't. It scared me too much to be open like that. Just like he was scaring me.

He stepped close to me and whispered in my ear, "In no time, I could have you shouting my name."

"Fuck you," I said though it did entice me. "If this is your approach, it's very lacking."

"Lacking?" he said quietly. "But this is the way we do it here, Nina."

I balled up my fist, ready to punch him. Instead, I pushed him away and said, "Well, in America we don't do it like that."

"Oh America," he said. "Such a kinky place. Well, what do you expect with such rampant repression?"

Again, with the condescension. I was so going to slap him.

He slid his finger down my cheek. "What's this here? A little bruise where you fell?"

I slapped his hand away from my face. "What are you getting at, François?"

"You know what I'm getting at," he said leaned in close again, then whispered, "Have you in your whole life lost any control?"

"Fuck you."

"In time," he said, nodding. "In time."

"I'd rather die than let you touch me," I said. But I was dying for it. I don't know how it happened, or why I wanted it, but I did. Something in me just seemed to change, like a switch had been flipped. I wanted him to come on, to get on with it. I was suddenly turned on by him. I wanted him to love me, fuck me, just do it and get it over with. I was ready to move forward but I needed a little push. He supplied it without hesitation.

He smiled and said, "No, you wouldn't."

I glared at him and suddenly felt the walls closing in on me. *I have to get out of here*, I thought. I didn't know this guy. He could be a psychopath for all I knew. I had to leave and I had to leave now. Without another word, I ran out, ran all the way down the street. I thought about taking a taxi. I couldn't afford a taxi all the way into Paris as I'd left most of my money at the apartment. Merde! I guess I hadn't counted on meeting some strange French man who'd take me to his Château outside of Paris. I'd have to find a Metro station.

So, I kept walking and walking until I found a little town and then the Metro. Once I was on, I sat down in the back. When I realized I'd left my bicycle there, I burst into tears.

Little Slut

"Oh, there you are," François said as soon as he opened his front door the next day.

"I want my bicycle back," I said.

"Certainly," he said and moved aside, waving me in with his hand. "Come in?"

"No," I said. "I just want my bicycle back. That's all. Get it for me."

"It's in the garage," he said and pointed to an old carriage house that had been converted into a garage probably about fifty years earlier. "Come with me."

I followed him to the garage and he went in and then came back out with my bicycle. The front tire was flat.

"Sorry about the tire," he said. "Want me to pump it up for you?"

"No," I said. "I'll just push it."

"You can't push it," he said. "Let me take you home."

"No," I said. "I just came for my bike."

He stood back from me, pulled a pack of cigarettes out of his shirt pocket and lit one. He offered me the pack, I declined, then he slipped them back into the pocket. Finally, he said, "You and I both know that you didn't come back for the bike, Nina."

"Sorry, but you're wrong."

He shook his head. "Let's have a coffee."

"No," I said. "I just want to leave."

He stared at me, the wheels in his mind obviously turning. He was onto me. I should leave. I should leave now.

"Come with me," he said and walked towards the house, flicking his cigarette away.

I watched him, then glanced at the still burning cigarette on the gravel drive. I sighed, walked over and squashed it out with my foot, then followed him into the house, down the hall and into the kitchen. Unlike the rest of the house, this was the only room that had been renovated. There were new stainless steel appliances, including a six-burner gas stove, very modern and expensive looking cabinets with white marble countertops, all sitting atop an old worn and beautiful red tile floor. The walls were painted in a fresh, bright white. It was a beautiful chef's kitchen.

"I like to cook," he said.

He liked to cook? I liked to cook, too. We had a commonality. So what? He was still an asshole.

He went over to the counter and poured coffee into two white cups. "I know it is not in character with the rest of the house, but so what? I like my modern conveniences."

"I see that," I said and sat down at the old, rustic French table which was long and rectangular. It shouldn't go with the modern room, but it did. He had taste. He knew what he liked. The chairs were vintage steel and wood, like they had been used in a factory of some sort and had been repurposed. They looked like they cost a fortune.

He walked over and placed a cup in front of me. I didn't touch it. I'd already had a coffee that morning and if I had any more, I'd be shaking like a leaf during a storm.

"I know what you want," he said and sat down. "You don't even have to ask."

"And what do I want?"

"Sex," he said matter-of-factly. "But not only that, you want to be punished."

Holy shit! He didn't just come out and say that, did he? Oh, yeah, he had. He was so blunt. So in your face. No beating around the bush for this one. I didn't know if I could handle such forthrightness. I was more into subtleties than that.

He had told me not only did I want sex, but that I also wanted to be punished. Punished for what? For wanting it? Sex? I shook my head, willing something to make sense but nothing did. And, yet, it was obvious. I did want sex and I wanted it from him. But the punishment thing? What was that about? I didn't know but I sure wasn't about to admit to anything.

I leaned back and crossed my arms, staring at him. He was so good looking, so eloquent. He was a dream man, *any* woman's dream man. He was perfect, tall, broad-shouldered, strong looking. He had the handsome face of a movie star, the body of a Greek god. He was the sort of man I wanted to have sex with, had always dreamed about having sex with. He would both ravish me and keep me safe. I knew that. I don't know how I knew that, but I did.

However, I couldn't tell him these things. He would think I was a fool, some romantic, silly American. I had to be cool and I had to not let on that I wanted what he obviously wanted to give me. So, I said, "I do not want sex from you and certainly not punishment. Whatever that means."

He nodded. "Of course, you do. You want sex and you want to be punished for wanting it. You want me to fuck you, then spank you afterwards. Or spank you, then fuck you."

"You are out of your damn mind," I said.

"Come on," he said and leaned in towards me. "It's always sex with you, isn't it? You're a little slut. Well, you are at least in your mind. That's why you never cheated on your husband. You couldn't give yourself permission to need what is human to want."

"Fuck you," I said and stood up. He was going too far. What the hell was this guy's problem? I didn't ask, though, because I didn't want to know. I was afraid there might be something slightly dangerous about him and I didn't know if I could handle it. I knew I'd picked him to do this but the thought of him not being quite right did cross my mind.

He grabbed my arm and gently forced me back into the seat, then released me. "Just sit and tell me. Isn't that what you want? You want sex and you want to be punished for wanting it so bad, like I said. Confirm my suspicions."

I blushed but he was right. Suspicions confirmed! That's why I was here and I was here because I thought he'd give it to me. I just didn't want to get hurt in the process.

"Am I right?" he asked.

I bit my bottom lip and nodded. I was so embarrassed, I wished the floor would swallow me up. I knew I could have not come back for the bike. It wasn't really worth anything and I could easily get another. I didn't abandon it because I wanted to see where he could take me. I wanted to see if my hunch about him was right. I wanted to know if he was the man who could give me what I wanted the most.

"Little sluts need to be punished," he said. "You want to be punished?"

Well, if we were going to do this, we might as well get started. I was tired of waiting for something to happen or watching as something passed me by that I could have easily grabbed a hold of. It was time for me to take life by the horns and it was time for me to allow this man to call the shots.

"Nina?" he said softly. "Answer me. You want to be punished?"

I bit my bottom lip and nodded again.

"Come over here then."

I stood and walked over to him. He looked up at me and began to touch me. I shivered with delight as he ran his hand up my legs and to my breasts.

"Take off your clothes," he said.

"What?" I asked.

"You heard me."

A bit of hesitation swelled up in my chest, but I pushed it away. Yes, I needed this. I had to see if I could do it. I had to prove to myself that it was what I wanted. I wanted to know if he could give it to me. I looked down at my outfit— an oversized but stylish black cashmere sweater, skinny jeans that were well worn in and fit my petite but trim body like a glove and black leather motorcycle boots that I wore over the jeans. It was the sort of outfit I wore almost every day of the week. It made me look young, hip, stylish and like I didn't give a shit. And it attracted a certain type of man, a man like François.

"Now," he said. "I want to see your body."

I started to say something, to tell him off. Again, getting caught up in the bullshit that always kept me from getting what I wanted. It was the inhibition, the anger that always stepped in and ruined it. But I realized I was doing this just because I thought that's what I *should* do. But I didn't. I couldn't utter a word. And I couldn't because I wanted to do what he wanted me to do. I wanted to lose control; I wanted him to have it.

"Would you like me to help?" he asked.

I didn't know. I just stared at him. It was like I was there, right there, ready to cross the line, ready to get the show on the road but something kept tripping me up and stopping me.

"Nina?" he said softly. "We both know you're going to do this."

He was right. I was going to do it. Maybe with just a little more prodding. I stared into his eyes, so dark and gorgeous, his eyelashes so full. The eyes stared at me, through me, into my soul. They were telling me they knew, just knew, what I wanted and what I needed. They told me he was the man to give it to me, down the last detail.

"It's been a while for you, hasn't it?" he asked. "A while since you last had sex, oui?"

I nodded but didn't say a word.

"A woman has needs just like a man," he said. "I can help you with this, Nina. I want to touch you everywhere and feel your skin. I want to kiss you and show you how it feels to be wanted."

I closed my eyes and thought about that. *To be wanted...* Isn't that what we all wanted? What we all needed? Even though I drove my husband away, I knew he wanted me. He just left because he finally gave up the fight.

"I want to see you naked," he said softly. "Show me your body. I want to see it. Do you understand?"

Did I? Did I understand? Yes, I did.

"Are you ready?" he asked.

I could tell he was. I could see the outline of his hard penis through his pants. He was ready. He was willing. He was able. He wanted me to want him. It was that simple.

"Then do it now."

Now. Right now. Not later. Just now. It was time. Could I do this? Could I undress and expose myself in front of a man I'd just met yesterday? Yes, I could. Easily. I wanted to. I wanted him to see me, every single square inch of my body. I hadn't stopped thinking about him since I'd run out of here yesterday. I was ready. I was willing. I was able. It was time.

I nodded and stepped back and pulled my sweater over my head, then pulled off my boots and socks. I glanced down at my toenails, which I'd painted the previous night while sitting on the side of the tub. They were cherry red and, as I'd painted them, I had fantasized about François taking notice of them, commenting on how lovely they looked. Then I caught myself doing this and stopped. *What was wrong with me?* I chastised myself, told myself I'd never see him again and that he was an asshole.

But I knew that wasn't going to happen. I'd even gone to sleep thinking about him and about what he could do to me. As I thought about this, I found my hands in my panties, rubbing myself, bringing myself to orgasm. I hadn't done that in a while. But he brought it out in me. I was suddenly fantasizing about his hands on me, on my naked skin, his lips devouring me, sucking my nipple, his tongue thrusting into my open, wet and willing mouth. I'd thought so much about him, I didn't fall asleep until late in the night. When I awoke, I was alive with this new feeling, this feeling of lust I'd never quite experienced before.

And now here I was, waiting on him to tell me my next move. And I loved it. *I loved it.* I was getting so turned on, so worked up, I was almost beside myself. *Just touch me*, I thought. *Just once, just touch me.* I needed it so badly I was on the verge of begging for it. But I didn't. I couldn't. It was his call to make and we both knew it.

He watched me, then took a good look at my breasts which were now heaving in my bra. He liked what he saw. But I shouldn't have even been doing this. I should probably just leave. It was going somewhere and if I didn't pull the plug soon, there would be no stopping it. But that didn't stop me. I wanted to do it. I wanted to see if I had it in me to do it. I needed it, so badly.

He motioned with one finger for me to take off my jeans. I did so and stood in my panties and bra. Yeah, they matched. They were an expensive tartan plaid set that made my body look so, so good. I had bought them a few weeks earlier at a fancy little Parisian lingerie boutique. I never wore anything like this and, after I purchased them, I wondered what the hell I'd been thinking, preferring comfortable boy shorts and simple underwire bras. I'd put them in a drawer and forgot about them until this morning when I knew I'd see François. Maybe it was kismet or something that I'd had the forethought to buy fancy lingerie and this was the sort of lingerie that would impress anyone. As I pulled the lingerie on, I had imagined him taking it off. Right then, I was waiting for him to do just that.

He couldn't contain his smile, then muttered, "Oh, lassie," in a faux Sean Connery Scottish accent.

I almost laughed but blushed instead. I also took note that he liked what he saw. Good. He should have.

His smile disappeared and then he paused for a long moment, his eyes skimming my body, not leaving an inch overlooked. I could tell me liked what he saw. I worked hard to keep my body looking good, toned and tight. My breasts were a firm C-cup and suited the frame of my body well. I had a body men lusted after and I knew it, even though I covered it up with baggy sweaters most of the time. I kept it like this just in case I ever met someone I'd want to show it off to. I was glad I had put forth the effort. I could tell he appreciated it, too.

Without a word, he leaned over and pulled me to him. I stood there and waited breathlessly for what he was about to do. It didn't take long before the tip of his finger went under my panties then tugged at them. I turned around and both his hands grabbed my ass, then his hands were under the panties, touching my bare ass. He squeezed it hard, then leaned in and kissed the small of my back just once.

A moan escaped my lips. I was getting heated up. I was finally going to get what I wanted, what I had been so horny for.

Then he tugged at my panties until they came off my body. My bare ass was in his face. I felt so vulnerable but I couldn't have moved if I wanted to. I wanted this. His hands played with my buttocks for a moment, then he sensuously but firmly kneaded them with his hands, squeezing so tightly I just knew he'd leave marks. But I didn't care about that. I just wanted to see what he would do with me offering myself like that.

I was about to find out. Before I could blink, his hand came down hard on my ass, thusly spanking me. He'd told me this was what I wanted. Was it? My ass burned as did my face. It was slightly humiliating, but then it wasn't. It was…*nice*. It felt good. I wanted more. Should I ask for another or would he automatically call the shots? I didn't know and I didn't have time to ask because he gave me another good smack on my other ass cheek. Then he squeezed both of them with both hands.

Was that all? Was there more where that came from? No. he was moving onto other things. His hand went in sideways between my ass cheeks, then down and down until it was sliding backwards and forwards on my pussy. Ahhh… That felt so damned good! Backwards and forwards… And then he paused on my clit and stopped moving, as if inviting me to pleasure myself with his hand. And I did. I found myself rubbing against his hand, feeling my juices began to flow, wanting to orgasm but waiting, waiting, waiting to do so; making the sensations last, feeling the wet softness of my cunt against his hand.

Before I could really get my groove on, he removed his hand and, out of nowhere, he gave my bare ass another good, hard smack. Back to the spanking. Wow. This almost jolted me back to reality, but something about it made me moan. Wow! What was he doing? Would he do more? In answer to my question, he gave me another good, hard spank, which almost sent me over the edge. I was so hot with lust for him, I could barely breath. Then I realized what this was. It was building anticipation. It was making me want him so badly I couldn't think straight. And want him I did. I was about to beg him to fuck me when he changed course again.

He started fingering me, touching me, teasing me. Lightly, lightly, lightly. Nothing too harsh or too insensitive. But, still, it was overwhelming. It was almost too much to bear, too much to take. Soon, I felt nothing but a flood of passion and intense heat spread through my body. I wanted to take his hand and bite at it, suck his fingers into my mouth and taste myself on him. But I didn't move. There was something about not seeing his face and not knowing what he was going to do that made me just want to go along with what was happening

He slid his hand in sideways again and rested it on my clit. Oh, yes. Now I could get it. And so, I did. I started going for it. Moving my slick, wet pussy against his hand. As I moved against his hand, his other hand grabbed my ass cheek again and squeezed. He leaned down again and kissed the small of my back, taking time to lick it just a little. And that's all I needed. I came from the visual of his tongue on my naked back and from the pressure of his hand on my clit.

I came for a good minute, a soft yet deep moan escaping my lips. I shuddered with the orgasm and once it was over, I wanted to climb on him, stick his cock in my pussy and ride the hell out of it.

When I came back down from the cloud of orgasm, I suddenly realized I was almost naked in front of this man. And he'd just made me come. He'd given me one of the best orgasms of my life and that made me feel just a little peculiar. It made me feel so vulnerable, almost weak. Once it was over, I felt a sudden flash of embarrassment. I didn't like that feeling. Why was I feeling *this* after *that*? I had to get out of there. I was leaving and I wasn't coming back. Yeah, that was what I was going to do. No more of this, of whatever this was. I was done. Right? I was done.

Before I could change my mind, I grabbed for my jeans, but he was on me in a second flat. He had me bent over the kitchen table and my legs spread wide. He wanted me now. He'd done the work and now it was his turn to play.

"Uh uh uh," he said. "Not so soon, my love. We have to finish what we started."

I didn't speak. I couldn't. I just wanted him. My embarrassment disappeared as my hands clawed the rough wood of the table and my breathing picked up. *This was it.* I wasn't leaving, after all. No. He was right. We had to finish what we started. The slight shame and vulnerability I'd felt earlier had disappeared and now I was ready to take what he was going to give. I was glad he had been quick and hadn't allowed me to flee. Yes, I was skittish, that much was true. What was truer was that I needed him to show me the way.

"Are you ready?" he asked, his breath on my back as he leaned heavily against me.

"Yes," I replied breathlessly, not wanting to talk, not wanting him to talk, just wanting to get fucked. Show me what you can do, you bastard! Just show me! Stick your hard cock in me, fill me up and fuck me good! I didn't say these things and I didn't say these things because I didn't have to. It was that intense. I knew he would soon be in me, fucking me from behind, with me taking it, wanting it, shouting his name, just like he said.

And I was.

The next thing I knew, his pants were around his ankles and his hard, wide and thick cock was in me, filling up my pussy and taking me over completely. It was almost too much to bear. It was so big, so big that I wondered for a second if it were real. I'd never had a cock this big—ever. He had to be at least eight, if not nine, long inches. Not only that, his cock was wide, which was the best part. It allowed me to really grab hold of it and ride it for all it was worth. It was like I receiving a gift I never knew I wanted but, once I had it, the realization of how much I'd been missing out on saddened me. I knew there was no going back after having this.

He reached around and grabbed my tits. I rose up to allow him more access and his hand went under my bra— the one item of clothing I'd yet to remove. But that didn't matter. Having that one little item of clothing on added to the sheer intensity of what he was doing to me—fucking me hard—and made it all the more enticing. It made me feel even more naked than I would have had I been completely without clothing. He squeezed my breasts hard and then fingered the nipples which sent me into a passionate tizzy. *More, more, more!* I wanted to shout this at the top of my lungs. I could not get enough. As we fucked, I wondered what I'd been waiting for. Why I hadn't done something like this sooner? Then I realized it was because I had been waiting on him, someone that would know perfectly well what I wanted and how to give it to me.

His hand went into my hair and slipped my ponytail holder out. My hair fell against my back. He pushed it to the side and pressed his face in my neck, which he sucked and licked. I shivered with delight at the sensation, loving every second of it. I moaned as he fucked me like this, as he fucked me dirty. I pressed back onto him, grinding it out, getting everything I could out of it and never wanting it to end. But, before I knew it, I was coming again. I came hard and fast and so did he, thrusting with all his might into me as he came inside of me. Then he collapsed on my back, breathing hard. I was breathing hard, too. It was like the wind had been knocked out of me. I was exhausted which meant it had been really, really good.

I didn't move for a good few minutes. Neither did he. Then he turned me around and pushed me up on the table and kissed me. It was our first kiss and it had come only after we'd fucked. I didn't pause to take that in. What that meant didn't matter and it didn't matter because this was no ordinary kiss. This kiss was deep, lust-driven and real. He licked at my lips before pushing his sweet tongue into my mouth. I sucked at his lips, at his tongue, eating at his mouth as my heart began to pound with lust again. His hands went down to my chest and touched it slightly, then his tongue dragged along my neck until it was near my breasts. Oh, yes. More, please. More of that. *Now!* His hand slipped under the strap of my bra and pulled it down until my breast was exposed, as my hard and erect nipple pointed at him and demanded attention. He bent down and licked that hard nipple slightly, then sucked it as hard as he could into his mouth.

"Ummm…" I moaned. "Oh, God, yes! Ummm…"

His other hand squeezed my other breast for a minute before slipping down to my legs, which were closed. He slipped his hand between them and I opened them wide for him. Then he began to just finger me, slipping his hand into my vagina while his thumb rested on my clit. I was about to come again. I knew this was possible, having multi-orgasms, but I didn't know how it would feel if it happened to me. I guess one just needs the right stimulation. And he was giving me that in droves.

François didn't move until I came again and I came hard. It was like there were fireworks exploding in my body, one right after the other. I shuddered with the orgasm and my head fell on his shoulder. It took me a minute or two to catch my breath.

Wow! Oh, wow! I'd never had anything like that in my life. It was so good and so dirty and just felt so right. Once again, for a moment, I almost felt shame; it was that good. But I wasn't ashamed. Something changed in me that day. Something shifted. Maybe having sex like that was the ticket out of my repression. Maybe having sex with him did it. I didn't care which, I just wanted more where that came from.

He turned away from me for a moment and pulled his pants up, zipping them. I stared at him, then down at my body, so naked and so vulnerable. I should probably get dressed, too.

But then I heard something outside, the sound of an approaching storm. This made me start and the sound brought us back to reality. We stared into each other's eyes for a moment, then I glanced at the window.

"Is that thunder?"

He nodded. "Are you afraid?"

I gave a slight shrug without looking at him then pushed him away and went to the window. The sky was dark. It looked almost foreboding. "Whenever it would storm, my mother would wake us up and take us into the basement," I said for some reason. "She was terrified of storms; afraid our house would get blown away by a big wind or something. She would shake with terror because my dad would usually be gone on the road. He was a truck driver."

I heard him coming towards me but I didn't turn around. I knew he was coming for me, to me. Once more. I didn't know if I could handle it again so soon. But instead of making a move, he simply put his arms around me and gave me a gentle squeeze, which baffled me. *What was up with him?*

When he pulled away, I realized this was a bad, bad idea. Having sex like this could only lead to one thing—me getting hurt and ending up with a broken heart. François was the kind of man women only dream about. I would soon find out about him and he'd disappointment me. He'd either cheat or, worse, lose interest and then where would I be? I'd be embarrassed, humiliated. I'd probably start obsessing about him or something. And that would be pathetic. No, I couldn't let him have my heart, no way. Girls like me don't end up with men like him. We just don't. He was a dream and I needed to get back to reality. I told myself that I'd had my fun and that's all I needed. I didn't want to get entangled in something I might not be able to get out of.

"Come back tomorrow," he said, staring at me. "We'll try something new."

"I'm not coming back," I said.

"Why not?"

"This is all I wanted," I said.

He chuckled and chucked me under the chin. "You know that you want more than that."

I glared at him.

"When you get home, you'll want it even more than you did before," he said, stepping in close to me. "You'll have to have it."

He just knew everything, didn't he? And knowing that pissed me off. Was I that obvious? Did he think that way about me? I was so pissed off at him then but mostly at myself for needing him like I knew I was going to. I was afraid of the need that he had awakened. I had put myself in a cage of self-doubt and was afraid to come out of it. Now he was making me leave it and I didn't like it one bit.

"I won't be back," I said and started to dress.

"Stay."

I ignored him and got dressed hastily. I had to get out of that place. There was a new side of me emerging and it was scaring me. I needed to be alone for a minute to gather myself, to pick apart my thoughts. I reached for my boots and started out.

"No," he muttered and his voice changed, just like that. "You won't go."

I ignored him and headed to the door but the tone of his voice sent shivers up and down my spine and my feet hesitated. François was a stranger. Sort of. Sure we'd had sex but I didn't know him and I sure didn't like the effect he was having on me. I could envision myself weeping over him like a schoolgirl over a picture of her favorite pop star. That didn't set well with me. I didn't like to show weakness and if he knew what he was doing to me, he might try to use it to his advantage.

"Stop," he said as soon as my hand was on the door knob.

"What is it?" I snapped and whirled around. "What do you want? We're finished here, okay? Done."

He shook his head. "No, we are not done. Not yet. Not today."

"Fuck you," I said and started to turn around.

He took three steps and was on me. I started to scream at him, to tell him to stop, but his hand came up and gave me a slight touch on my lower back.

"I will not lose you today," he whispered in my ear.

"What does that mean?"

"Stop running from me," he said softly, pushing my hair back and pressing his face into my neck.

"No. François," I murmured, though I didn't want him to stop. "Don't."

"Shh," he said.

"No," I said and pushed him away.

He stared at me, then stepped in to me and pushed his heavy body onto mine. I started to push back, but found myself pushing into him, moving with him, pressing against him.

He grabbed the back of my head and pulled it back so that my lips were near his. Then he gave me a hard kiss, thrusting his tongue into my mouth. He was going to give it to me again, this time rough. It was like this brutish side of him suddenly appeared out of nowhere and he was going to make sure he had control of not only the situation but of me, as well. Control me? No. No way. That infuriated me. I felt myself wanting to hurt him, wanting to push him away, but then he just held me tightly, not letting me move. I pushed against him but he held his embrace. I stopped moving and felt it, felt him next to me, so close. Then something in me just broke and I felt... I felt... Oh. God. Something just took me over and I felt *lust*. Again. I just felt it. Maybe I brought that out in him. I don't think it was there before. Maybe he brought it out in me, but it was a hunger, a need we both shared that came to the surface. It frightened me but at the same time, I couldn't get enough. His need was to dominate. My need was to submit. It went along together like peanut butter and jelly.

We slid down to the floor, out lips locked. Then he paused and that made me pause. He pressed his forehead to mine, like he was going to make sure I didn't look away. Then he pushed my sweater up and his hand slipped into my bra. He grabbed the top of it and pulled it down so my breast popped out. I started to moan. It was almost too much. It was almost too soon. But then... Then he tore off my clothes, throwing them over his head and to the side as his hands desperately tried to get to my naked skin. Soon, I was naked. And I wanted him naked, too. I tore at his clothes, literally ripping them off his body until he was as naked as me. I paused for a moment to take in his body. It was beautiful, long, lean and muscular. He was perfect. I wanted him more than ever so I grabbed him and pulled him on top of me, pressing my naked body into his. It felt *so good*.

And then we were fucking.

Soon, my legs were wrapped round his waist and I was getting the most out of our fuck. It was a long, hot, sweaty one. The rain began to beat down, just right outside where we were. I was so spent I was almost shaking with exhaustion. But I couldn't stop. I'd never had so much sex in my life. But it felt right, like something you're supposed to do on a rainy afternoon.

This time, it was all about doing it, fucking. We didn't kiss and we didn't grope, we just fucked. He fucked me like that, not blinking. Our eyes connected and locked, unflinching uninhibited. But it didn't last. We were too wound up for that. We were so wound up, we were about to explode just from the overload of lust in our bodies for each other. It wasn't long before we both came, almost simultaneously. As we came, he pulled out and came all over my chest and tits. That's when I grabbed him and pulled his mouth on top of mine and ate at him. We kept kissing until we finally came back down from the fucking.

Once it was over I got up, got dressed and prepared to leave. He didn't say a word and neither did I. There wasn't much to talk about, not after you spend time like that with someone. It was a done deal. And it was over.

So, I ran off again. I found myself on the Metro, then walking back to the apartment beneath the Parisian sky, almost crying, wondering what the hell I was doing and where the hell this might lead. I was afraid of losing myself in him and I was afraid because he might end up hurting me, way more than my ex-husband ever thought to. François was a man you didn't just love, but a man you fell in love with and that love would drive you crazy. It would be a possessive love and I was not a possessive person. This new part of me that he was bringing out scared me. I didn't like it and I didn't want to get wrapped up in it.

When I opened the door to my apartment, James looked up at me from the couch. "Where the hell have you been?"

I shrugged. Even though we shared everything, I would never share this with anyone, not even my best friend. Besides, what would I tell him? That I wanted this man to take me over, to take control, to fuck me silly? While I wasn't a prude, I sure wasn't an exhibitionist, nor a braggart. I would never flaunt anything, not something so sexual and personal.

He eyed me and said, "And where the hell is your bicycle?"

I groaned.

"Oh, well," he said then jerked his head towards an enormous bouquet of red roses. "At least tell me who those are from."

I gasped at the sight of the roses, at the enormity of the bouquet. It was *gorgeous*. Of course, I knew who they were from. When I read the card, all it said was, "Any time."

"What does that mean?" James asked.

I shrugged.

"Do you have a boyfriend?"

"Not really," I said, refusing to share. "It's just some guy I met in a café. We went to…dinner. I mean lunch. We had lunch."

He nodded. "It must have been one helluva lunch," he said and picked up a red box and handed it to me. "This came, too."

I stared at him and opened it up. It was a beautiful stainless steel tank watch from Cartier. From Cartier! It was heavy and looked like it cost a fortune. I glanced at the note again: "Any. Time," and smiled. I got it. Quite clever, François.

"Try it on," he said.

I took the watch out of the box and slipped it on, then shook my arm, moving it around before letting it fall to my wrist. "That's really cool." I smiled at him. "Like it?"

He nodded. "Obviously someone likes you."

Yeah, I guess he did.

He grabbed my arm and took a good look at the watch, shaking his head, then whistled under his breath, "Whew! Are you fucking kidding me? What the hell did you do to this guy?"

That was a good question.

How Do You Like It?

"You like that, don't you?" François asked softly.

I looked away from him and felt embarrassment wash over my cheeks, over my entire body. I was sitting in chair, waiting for what was coming next, anticipating it, wanting it. I wanted it so much I almost dreaded its arrival out of fear that I might be disappointed.

"Don't you?" he whispered closer to my ear.

I could deny it. I could run. I could run so far away I would never see his face again. His handsome, bordering on beautiful face. His French mannerisms. His dark hair and his dark eyes. I could run but no matter how far away I got, he would forever be imbedded in my consciousness, like a memory of something you lost once and never found again. I'd had that happen before. It was a silver bracelet my father had bought me when he'd been away on the road. The first time I wore it to school, it fell off my wrist and I never found it again. Anytime I thought about that bracelet—and how special it was to me, mainly because my father was the one who had given it to me—I got a terrible ache in my stomach. *What had happened to it?* I'd never know and that drove me crazy. I just didn't know if I could deal with having François in my memory like that.

I stared at his face and still couldn't get over how good looking he was. It was almost as if he wasn't real. We'd been at this a while now, at least a few weeks, and each time was more intense than the last. And he kept looking better.

"Yes, you do," he said, assuring himself, and me, of his assertion. "You like that."

He stepped back and nodded at me and then I knew he had me completely figured out. He knew why I had come here even though last time I vowed would be my last. And the time before that and the time before that... But I'd been coming to him for a few weeks now. Every single time we met, we fucked like crazy and when we finished, I would get up and race out of his home like some crazy person. Why I was playing this foolish game was beyond me. But played it I did. I would show up, we would exchange a few words, pleasantries mostly like, "Nice weather we're having," or "Here, try some of this wine. It is delicious." And then we would start having sex. It would begin with his giving my cheek a slight graze with the back of his hand or me stepping in towards him. Then he would grab me, I would grab back and we would fuck ourselves silly.

The only annoying part was my issue with staying after we were done having sex. It probably annoyed him, too, but he never called me out on it. He said once, "I believe one day we will have dinner together, Nina."

We still hadn't gotten to it. I didn't know if we ever would. He kept promising to cook for me, and I for him, but it never came to that. I'd leave quickly, I'd get home and ever so often, I'd find another gift from him. Sometimes gorgeous flowers, sometimes expensive luxury items like the quilted Chanel bag I'd gotten three days ago and sometimes jewelry, like the Cartier watch. All gifts to show me… What exactly? What was the message? I didn't know but I would wear the jewelry, smell the flowers and carry the bags. And I wore the watch every day. He would notice, give me a slight smile and then smooth the hair back from my face to stare at a pair of earrings. "Yes," he would say. "They do suit you very well."

I tried not to put too much into it.

Today, I was wearing a necklace. The chain was diamonds and the pendant was sapphire. He had pulled down my sweater to stare at the necklace, then ran his finger up my chest, then back down. He nodded with approval and turned away from me. That's when I knew something else was going on and that today would be different. I didn't know what it was but something had changed, shifted in the room, in the atmosphere. It was all different now. He was different. I was different. There was no denying it.

He went behind me and grabbed hold of my shoulders with his hands. I shivered with anticipation. *What was he going to do?*

"You said you would never come back," he told me without moving. "Why did you return?"

This was our game. We didn't play it every day, but we played it enough. He knew why I had returned. The question was too obvious to answer.

I swallowed hard as a lump came up in my throat. I hated myself for an instant before I started to hate him and that made me want to cry. He had me in a twist, that's all I could say. I suppose I hated the fact that I was so obvious, that he had me figured out and made me go through this slight interrogation before he'd give me what I'd come for— sex. He knew I wanted him and he knew I would return. Each time, I wanted him worse than the time before that. But I couldn't let him know that. That would be showing weakness and to show weakness now… Well, that would be the deal-breaker. We had to go through the game to get to the sex.

"Tell me," he said and squeezed my shoulders.

"Please," I muttered. "Don't."

"But you want it," he said and added, "Again."

I hung my head in shame.

"You want it and you want me to give it to you," he said, coming around to face me. "If I did not give it to you, would you find another man who would?"

I shook my head.

"No?"

"No," I muttered.

He bent a little at the waist and pointed at me with his finger. "I think you are lying."

"I'm not lying."

"You are."

I shook my head in protest but his hand came up to silence me, silence my actions.

"I'll give you what you think you want and stop doing this. I'll leave you alone. I will not do this again."

"But, but—"

The hand came up again. I bit my tongue and waited.

"No," he said. "I won't."

"Why not?" I cried.

"You enjoy it too much," he said.

Wasn't that the point of it? I remained silent, nevertheless. I remained silent because I knew he was going to give it to me. Eventually. He was just teasing me, making me beg. I could beg for it. Men begged for sex all the time, didn't they? What was so wrong with a woman doing it every once in a while? *Why not?*

I looked around the room. We were in his bedroom. I took in the big upholstered Louis XV French Provincial bed, the oversized armoire, the well-worn Persian rug on the floor. The room was dark. He'd closed the heavy silk curtains when we entered. The walls were painted a soft, light green. It was color you didn't see much anymore but was so lovely it made me want to fall asleep in here, under the linen duvet and on the goose down pillows. But this wasn't about sleeping, not at all.

He got down on his knees in front of me. I breathed in his smell. He smelled divine and it wasn't cologne or soap or any of that. It was him; his smell that drove me crazy. It was a nice smell that was undetectable if you weren't close to him. But I was so close I could smell it. It made me want him even more.

"You do enjoy it, don't you?" he whispered softly.

"Yes."

He began to lean in towards me and I leaned in towards him. He pressed his face into my belly and then he looked up into my eyes. *What was he thinking?*

"Would you beg for it?" he whispered as I knew he eventually would.

"Of course," I whispered back.

He smiled and ducked his head. He liked this, this game, the first real one we'd ever played. It had been played before, but now it had been accelerated. Now, it had changed. I could feel it in the air. The last time had changed everything. The last time he told me he was getting bored and that soon I, too, would become bored with just the sex. It was time to do something different. It was time to up the ante. We were about to do just that. I couldn't wait, either.

"You're very bad," he told me. "You are so bad."

"I'm bad."

"Tell me how bad."

I sucked my lips into my mouth for an instant before responding, "So bad I would beg for it."

"For what?"

That was a good question. What was I begging for? I was begging for the excitement and the anticipation and the massive orgasm he'd helped me achieve. I was begging for him to give it to me, just like he did before.

"For you," I said.

He stood up and walked away from me. "Then you crawl."

"Excuse me?" I asked and almost laughed.

"Crawl," he said and waved his hand towards the floor. "Crawl over here towards me. Like a beast."

And here it was. Here it was in my lap. I could take it to the next level or I could be humiliated by it. By him. By his request. What was so hard about it? Did it put me on a lower level? Did it make me into something detestable? Something undesirable? No. That wasn't our game. Our game was to push each other, for him to push me and for me to be pushed. He wasn't trying to humiliate me and I understood that. He was trying to push me. Push all those preconceived notions out of my mind and make me understand something. What that something was, I didn't know. But it was something worth exploring.

I didn't even hesitate. I could do it, I could take it. I asked for it. This was what I really wanted. I wanted him to dominate me. I wanted him to tell me what to do, to command me to do things I would never do for another man. So, I slid down off the chair and got on all fours. I took my time positioning myself on the floor before I began to crawl towards him. I had to hide my smile in case he thought I wasn't taking this as seriously as he was. I took it slow, took my time as I made my way over to him, swaying my hips as I went.

"Stop."

I stopped.

He came over to me, bent down and kissed me. I responded by opening my mouth and a moan came out of me, from deep down inside. He licked at my lips before he slid his tongue in and then I sucked on it and he moaned with pleasure.

He stopped abruptly and stood up. I knew that was too easy.

"Now take off your shirt."

I sat up and began to unbutton it. It was a long sleeved white shirt. I'd gotten it on sale. It was a nice shirt but a bitch to iron. I wondered if he noticed how crisp it looked. Then I glanced down at my bare legs. My jeans were already off. I was just in my shirt and panties, another pair I'd purchased from the little boutique, this one in black lace. My credit card was going to be fat with lingerie, but I didn't care. I wanted to look good for him. I wanted him to think about how sexy my lingerie was. And when he thought about it, he'd think about me and that would make him want me even more, to know I'd taken the time to buy such things to please him.

"Wait."

I stopped just as I was sliding the shirt off my back. He came over to me again, bent down and cupped one of my breasts in his hand. He stared at my breast as he did so, then he moved away again and stared into my eyes.

"Tell me about the first man who fucked you."

"What?"

"You heard me."

I had heard him. I didn't know if I could talk about the first guy I had sex with as I didn't even like thinking about it. It was an embarrassing memory.

"Tell me about him," he said.

"He was young."

"Younger than you?"

"No," I said and shook my head. "Just young. Twenty. I was twenty, too. We were both virgins."

"So, you started late, with sex, I mean."

"I suppose I did."

"Did you orgasm?"

"No."

"Why not?"

"He came too quickly," I said.

"Did he get you off afterwards?"

"No," I said.

"Why not?"

"I didn't ask him to."

"Why?"

"I didn't feel…" I hesitated and stared at him. He nodded for me to continue so I said, "I didn't really know enough to ask."

"But he came?"

"Yes."

"So your pleasure was not worth…?" He snapped his fingers as if searching for the right word. "Not worth the trouble?"

"No, it wasn't that."

He got down in my face and said, "What was it?"

"I felt…embarrassed."

"Why?"

"Because it didn't feel right."

"Does this feel right?" he asked and traced a line on my arm.

I shivered and nodded.

"What is so different from this?" he asked and his hand moved to my breast. He squeezed it and I moaned. "Hmmm?"

"I don't know," I said and looked away from him and towards window. The curtains were still closed. I couldn't see if the sky was darkening or not. I didn't know what time it was or when I'd have to go home.

"You know," he said and pressed his face in my hair. "It is different because you want me and maybe you didn't want him. What was his name? This fellow who fucked you?"

"Charlie."

"You didn't want Charlie," he said. "But you want me. Am I right?"

"Yes."

"Tell me you want me."

"I want you."

"Tell me why."

I swallowed hard and noticed how excited I was. How wet. How much I desired him. I wanted to grab his hand and put it inside my panties. I wanted him to lick and kiss me down there, on my wet and swollen pussy. I wanted him so much I could have eaten him alive.

"I want you," I said and turned my head so our noses were touching. "Because you know what to do. You know what I want."

He smiled. He liked that.

"How do you want it?" he asked and pushed me gently down on the floor until I was on my back. "How would you like me to fuck you this time?"

"I don't care," I said and began to squirm. "Just do it."

"Now, now," he said and shook his head like a school marm. "I think you should wait longer."

"No," I moaned and grabbed his hand.

He pulled it back and shook his head. He was punishing me. Punishing me because I hadn't believed he had it in him. I hadn't believed he had the ability to do to me what I needed. He was reveling in his role as the dominate by making me wait. I almost hated him for it. But then I didn't.

He climbed on top of me and whispered, "I know what you like."

I breathed, "Yes?"

"You like this," he said and grabbed my crotch. "You like me to take you."

I gasped. "Yes."

"You like for me to be in control of you, of your body so that you have no say in what I do and you have to give yourself away."

"Yes," I moaned. "Do it."

He released me then he ripped the panties off my body and threw them to the side. Then his hand was playing with me, teasing me so much my hips rose up off the floor and I began to grind against his hand, which was doing the things to me that I loved and needed it to do.

"Ahh," I moaned and felt the orgasm.

"Not so fast," he said.

"Ahh," I moaned and grabbed his head, bringing his lips to mine. He tried to move away but I wasn't letting him budge. I wanted him right there, right then. I wanted him to take control and fuck me. It didn't take long before he obliged. Then he couldn't control himself. He was coming out of his pants and his hard cock was pressing against my leg. I grabbed onto it and stroked it. He pulled back and watched me. I stared into his eyes and then moved and took it in my mouth, giving it a good, hard suck as I did so. A deep moan came out of his mouth and he stroked my hair as I sucked his cock. I pulled back and kissed it with my lips and then licked it with my tongue. Then I put it back in my mouth and began to suck again, gently at first, then harder as I began to really get into it. I gripped his balls, giving them a slight squeeze, and once I did that, he almost came. This time it wasn't me about to lose control then, it was him.

He drew in his breath and pushed me back against the floor then fell on top of me, pushing my legs open with his. Then he entered me, going all the way in, hitting bottom as he did so. A small scream came out of my throat as he took me. Then he started fucking me, fucking me hard. My legs wrapped around his waist so he could get in even deeper, so I could have more of him.

His nose pushed my bra to the side and then his mouth found my nipple and he sucked it in while his other hand squeezed my breast hard. It was almost too much. I had to come and I had to come now, though the thought of not prolonging this fucking, this good fucking, was almost too much to bear. But he was fucking the orgasm out of my body and then it gripped me and made me shake and shimmy and shiver. Just as he was shaking and shivering. It was almost as if we were on fire. Once it was over, we lay there as the world came to an end and then started back up again.

It took a few seconds for me to get my breath back. When I got it, I couldn't help but smile at him. Now, that's what I was talking about.

"We will do this again," he said and kissed my cheek.

"You'll have to hurry," I said. "I have to be home in an hour to meet James."

He nodded.

"It's his birthday," I said and touched the side of his face. "I'm taking him out to dinner."

"Okay," he said.

I pulled back and stared at him.

"What is it?"

"I just realized that I know nothing about you. Not really."

He shrugged.

"Tell me something about yourself," I said.

"Why?"

"I want to know everything about you, that's why."

He stared at me and said, "There's nothing to know. You know everything you need to know."

That's what he was like. And that's exactly why I liked him.

Let the Games Begin

Just like that it turned from an affair into a game, into a part of my life. I began to desire him and wonder what he'd do next. I began to feel my sexual power, my sexual energy exploding inside me. I began to feel like a woman. Before, I never had time for anything like this. Now I did.

It was the tension—the anticipation—that made me hot. What would he do next? That was the most tantalizing part.

Now, he was taking a different route. We were in his bedroom again. I was in the same chair, waiting on him to begin. This time, he went to the armoire, opened it and pulled out a riding crop. What could *that* be for?

"Undress," he said.

I was about to, but then my curiosity got the best of me. "What's that for?"

He slapped it against his hand. "I used to ride, play polo. Do you like polo?"

I shrugged. I'd never given it a thought one way or another.

"You will like this," he said. "Undress, please."

I wasn't so sure. But when I was down to my panties and bra, he shook his head, indicating he wanted me all the way undressed. I complied and stood naked in front of him.

"Bend over the bed," he said.

Oh…okay. I went to the bed and bent over, my ass in front of him. He approached me but then stopped short just before he could touch me. Then I felt the crop making its way down my naked back and then down the crack of my ass. I shivered in delight. What was going to do with that thing?

I soon found out. He pulled back and cracked the crop against my ass. I screamed as it hit my skin. Then I felt the burn. I started to rise but then he said, "No, no, no." What? What did he mean *no*? He got up next to me and slid his hand down my other ass cheek, touching it softly, then gave it a hard crack with the crop. I screamed again as the pain seemed to bite into my soul.

Then there was silence.

Neither one of us moved or spoke for a long time, then he whispered, "Another?"

Another? Could I handle another? Something in me decided that, yes, I could. So I said, "Yes," breathlessly and he made contact again. And again. Each time, the crop bore into my skin and made it burn. Each time, I was brought closer and closer to ecstasy, closer to freedom.

Soon, my ass was on fire and the crop had been cast aside on the bed in front of me. François positioned himself behind me and slipped his hand around until it rested on my pussy. He began to move it, up and down, up and down. The juices from my pussy allowed his hand to slide easily. He stopped and then ran both hands up and down my ass cheeks before pulling them open and playing with my anus with one finger before he slipped it in.

Aahhh! *Ahhh*! I'd never had that, never had someone do something like that to me. I heard him unzip his pants then felt his hard cock slide between my ass cheeks until he positioned it for entry. I tensed in anticipation, in lust, wanting him to stick it in. He eased it in, inch by hard and thick inch, until he was fucking me, fucking me in the ass. I was still bent over the bed, my ass in the air, him taking me from behind, him fucking me like that, fucking me dirty. I didn't know what this felt like, this all encompassing feeling of true dirty lust, but it felt like nothing I'd ever had before and I never wanted it to stop.

As he fucked me, he pushed my legs open wider then reached around and grabbed the riding crop. He turned it around until the handle pointed at me and somehow—I don't know how—he slid it between my legs until it found my clit. *Ahhh*! I didn't know if I could stand much more of this. It was almost too much. I was going in overload. I began to ride to handle of the crop, feeling its slightly rough leather rub against my clit nicely. And so, I rode the crop and François rode me. We took our time. This fucking was slow and methodical. It was deep and intense, his hard cock in me like that and I clit-playing with the crop. It didn't take long before I began to come and as I came, I wailed a deep, long throaty wail with the orgasm. François pumped into me as my orgasm kept coming and coming then he pulled out and shot his load of hot come all over my back. I squirmed as it hit me, loving how it felt, how it slid down between my ass cheeks, the sheer dirtiness of it. I collapsed onto the bed, staring at the crop, as it seemed to stare back at me. The crop had beaten me in more ways than one. It would become a welcomed friend, I knew.

"Tonight," he said and kissed my naked shoulder. "You will stay for dinner."

There was no arguing with that. James would have to fend for himself.

Alive With Lust

It was like that. It was wonderful. It was the best time of my life. Every day, I would awake and begin to think about him. Some days, when he had business to attend to, we didn't meet and on those days, I would be alive with lust for him. I would obsess about the riding crop and what he would do with it. I loved not knowing. I loved what we were doing, how adult and how dirty it was. I loved that it was never tiresome and each time got better.

Like this time. It was one of the best. Or it was going to be. He was just about to crack the riding crop across my naked ass but then suddenly stopped. He took it away. I grabbed at it on instinct but he held it away from me. I huffed and tried to think of a way that would make him to do it.

"I want it," I said, unable to come up with anything better.

"No," he said.

I sighed with desire and impatience. "Please."

He grinned and motioned for me to turn over again. I smiled back and turned over, pushing my face into the mattress of the bed and raising my ass in the air. He brought it down across my ass. I shivered with delight. "Again."

He did it again, this time it would leave a mark that would be covered by my clothes that no would know about. But me. And him.

He turned me around and pressed his forehead to mine. We were like a pair of antelopes who press their heads together as they battle. He always did this when we fucked, as if he wanted to make sure I understood he was the dominant one. He didn't have to make sure. I gave him that privilege long before we played our first game.

Sometimes, I did think about what we were doing and why it turned me on so much. Was there a primary need in me to be punished? He took it when he wanted it. That's all that mattered to him. And getting it from me was where he wanted it from. He wasn't interested in doing any of this stuff with anyone else. Only me; I had been picked, I was his star, his fuck buddy, the woman who would run to the ends of the earth and back again for him.

Well, as long as he went with me, I mean.

He made everything in my life less important. Silly things I'd cried about no longer made me miserable. And I had been miserable for a long, long time.

Misery, like anything else, becomes a habit. There is a lot of safety in misery. It's almost comforting. I had spent a lot of time being afraid. But afraid of what? The unknown? The fear of being alone? What was the fear that bound me to him? I didn't know but it didn't matter too much. But I did know that the introduction of the riding crop had somehow disabled the fear. I was no longer afraid. I was free.

I loved to take what he gave to me, those hot, lusty and sweaty sex sessions but I always felt a little uneasy afterwards, as if I'd gotten something without getting approval first and I'd get punished later on for it. Which wasn't so bad.

Today was a different game. Today was the waiting game. He was doing everything to build up to the fuck. Delaying it, that's what he was doing. He moved away from me and walked around studying me like he'd studied the painting in the museum the first day we met.

"If you don't fuck me soon," I said. "I'll leave and fuck the first man I see on the street."

The smile slid off his face. "Don't ever say that."

I stared into his eyes. He was serious. The thought of me and another man drove him crazy, which meant only one thing. He loved me. And that sort of scared me. I knew he did but this proved it. If you don't love someone, you're not jealous with whom they spend time. And you certainly don't send them expensive gifts. Had he done that out of insecurity? Had he done that to buy my love? He never had to do that. Maybe he had done it to show me that he could do it, that he would do it, that he should do it. It wasn't so bad being on the receiving end of someone wanting to impress you, either.

"Does the thought of me fucking another man scare you, François?" I asked, really wanting to know though I already knew the truth.

He shook his head. "No, it angers me."

I loved it. I hated to admit it, but I loved knowing that he was jealous of me. He pushed me back on the bed and pushed my legs open with his knee. I went with him and we were just about to kiss when he pulled back.

"No," he said and moved off the bed. "I'll take you home."

"What?" I asked and sat up on my elbows, staring at him. "Are you serious?"

"Yes, I am," he replied. "Get dressed."

I shook my head. So, I wasn't going to get fucked, was I? Whatever. I decided I wasn't going to bitch at him and I wasn't going to do that because I had pushed him too far. Next time I would keep my mouth shut. Besides, I knew he wouldn't let me leave without at least a quickie. It was still early, still daylight. We still had *plenty* of time. I asked, "So, you'll drive me?"

"Oui."

"Good," I said. "I'm getting sick of the metro."

He nodded and we got dressed. I looked over at him and realized he was one-hundred percent mine. I didn't share anything about him with anyone, not even my roommate James, who I now rarely saw. All I told him was that I was having a storybook Parisian romance. He was glad for me as he was having one himself. I never even told him François's name or what he looked like. He was kept secret because I didn't want to give anything about our affair away to anyone else, not even a detail about it.

"Ready?" he asked and headed out the door.

I stared after him, then glanced at my watch. It was still early, so early that I wondered why he was doing this. We hadn't even had sex yet. And I hadn't come all the way out here not to get what I'd come for.

"François?" I called.

"Come, Nina," he called back. "We must go."

I stared after him. He was serious! So much for the quickie. I followed him down the stairs and out the door and then we took off in his car. But he didn't head back into Paris; he headed out, towards the country.

"Where are we going?" I asked and looked out at an open field full of fresh spring grass.

"For a drive," he said and took my hand and kissed it. "Would you like that?"

"Very much," I said and smiled at him. "Are you still mad at me?"

"A little," he said. "Let's not discuss."

Fine by me. We drove in silence for a while, then he stopped the car and pointed at a field which was surrounded by trees. "I want to fuck you there."

I turned to stare at it.

"Would you let me do that?"

I stared at him. "I don't think so, François."

"But I think you should," he whispered in my ear.

I looked away from him towards the field, then back. He smiled his most gracious smile and gave a little nod.

"I want you to get out and take off your clothes and wait for me."

I stared at him. "I can't do that."

"Try and see."

I looked at the field then at the road, which was pretty much deserted.

"Umm?" he said.

"Uh," I said, unable to think straight. "Uh…uh…"

"I think you would like it," he said and leaned over and slipped his under my sweater until he was squeezing my breast. "You will like it very much."

"Fran—"

"Shh," he murmured and played with my breast.

I squeezed my eyes shut as he did that.

"Go on now," he said and nudged me.

I took a breath and got out of the car. I looked back at him and he nodded for me to go on. I turned and walked towards the field, taking my jacket off and throwing it to the side. I turned back around to stare at him. He was watching me with a bemused smile. That smile gave me courage and I kept taking clothes off as I went deeper into the field. First my boots, then my jeans, my light sweater, my bra and then my panties. Then I turned to stare at the car, towards him. And I waited.

I was totally naked. I was totally vulnerable. I *loved* it.

It didn't take him ten seconds before he was out of the car and running towards me. My heart began to race and I began to feel so alive I thought I could fly into the blue sky above. He was there, suddenly, he was there and he was kissing me, touching my naked body as it pressed into his fully clothed one. I'd never felt as alive as I did then. I'd never felt as loved.

I grabbed into his ass and pulled him deeper into me. He walked me over and pushed me up against a tree. My mouth opened wide and grabbed onto his tongue, sucking on it, wanting it on my neck, then my breast, then my pussy. He pulled back and ran his tongue down my neck and then to my chest and then to my breast. He grabbed my arms and pushed them up over my head and then he ran his tongue down my underarm. A moan came out of my mouth. That felt so good.

His hands began to play with my breasts, squeeze them. Then he bent down and kissed each nipple once, before going back to the first to suck it into his mouth. Another moan came out of my lips, this one more intense.

He paused and pulled back a little, staring into my eyes. I stared back and watched his hand, flat and wide, as it slid down my naked chest, between my breasts and to the little bit of hair I didn't have waxed off and there it stopped and he ran his fingers into it, massaging me there, before his thumb slipped between my lips and found my clit.

"Ummm…" I moaned. "Oh, more, baby, more…"

He complied and kept his thumb there while his other finger began to play with my ass, slightly slipping into my hole while another one slipped into my cunt. My hips began to sway and I began to move slightly at the touch and before I knew it, this light, warm and welcoming orgasm opened up in me, much like a flower opens up during the first warm day of spring. I was in heaven. This was heaven.

I grabbed into his face, pulling it to me and sucked at his lips, biting at them with lust and need. I needed more of that, wherever it came from. I needed his hard cock inside of me.

He took his cue and pushed me down into the grass and climbed over me, then he began to kiss me, kiss my naked body, taking my nipple into his mouth and sucking on it. I moaned and arched up and grabbed onto his neck, pulling him down on me. I just wanted to fuck him now. I grabbed onto his belt and began to undo it. He helped and then I unzipped his pants and took his cock in my hand. It was hard and ready to fill me.

I pushed his pants down over his ass and wrapped my legs around his waist and his cock found its way into me. I let out a hiss of lust as he began to fuck me, ram into me with all his might. He was making me whole again, fucking me silly. I could not get enough of him. He couldn't get enough of me.

Then he paused. He stopped moving. My eyes fluttered open and I stared at him, into his eyes.

"What is it?" I asked breathlessly.

"I love you," he said and began to move again. "I love you very much, Nina."

A big smile came over my face. "I love you too, François."

He grinned and kissed me. I wrapped my arms around his neck and told myself I'd never let him go. It wasn't long before I felt the orgasm and I felt him coming, too. That made the fuck intensify and I was moaning loudly, with such intense satisfaction I thought I'd burst. When it was over, he gave me little kisses all over my face, on my eyelids, on the tip of my nose, on my lips. I lay there and wanted more.

When I opened my eyes, we smiled at each other. I thought, *He could make me do anything. Anything.* He was pushing me to make me feel emotions that had been lying dormant inside of me. They'd been asleep for so long and now they were being awakened. It was like I was being awakened. And I was. I cried with it whenever he fucked the orgasm out of my body. I screamed with the liberation he gave me when he brought the crop down against my bare ass. I moaned with it whenever he threw me up against the wall and took me. That's when I realized it's not about enslavement of the body; it's about enslavement of the heart. And once the heart is enslaved, there's no going back. And there was no going back for me. Not now, maybe not ever.

And, of course, that's when I panicked. That's when I knew I couldn't stay.

Better Left Unsaid

"Where are you going?" François asked and looked at the two small suitcases in the apartment hallway.

"You can't come in," I said and stopped him.

"Why not?" he asked. "I haven't heard from you in days."

"I'm sorry," I said. "I've been busy. It's been a year and James had already left. We're going back home."

Which was true, sort of. But James had been gone for about a month. I was just staying here until I worked up the nerve to leave François. To leave Paris, to leave it all behind. And I was leaving because I was scared. I knew how much I loved him and that scared me. I knew how much he loved me and that scared me even more. Why I was just coming to this conclusion was anyone's guess. I didn't know why love scared me like that. I guess I'd just never felt the intensity of it before. I didn't want to be consumed by it. And it was time to go home.

But the real reason? I was afraid our relationship might become too comfortable, too nice. I didn't want him to be so familiar that the sight of toothpaste in the sink in the morning would piss me off, the way it used to when my ex-husband did that. What we had was a dream and I didn't want to lose that feeling of passion. I knew I was just panicking. That's all. It's like I thought I *had* to run. And so, I followed that instinct though it was leading me to a great big nowhere.

"Where are you going?" he asked again.

"Home."

"Why?" he asked, his eyes full of concern.

"I can't do this anymore," I said. "Besides, I told you that I had to leave."

"No, you didn't."

It was true. I hadn't. I thought once that I should, but I didn't want to spoil the mood. I didn't want to hurt him, either.

"Are you angry with me?" he asked.

"No," I said. "It's just time I left."

"Why are you leaving?" he asked. "You don't have to leave."

"Yes, I do," I said.

"Tell me why."

"It's better left unsaid, François," I said and wished he wouldn't have come here. This was too hard. I had just wanted to run away without seeing him ever again. I had to go home. It was time. Besides, what else could I have done? Rented an apartment? Then I'd have to get a job... It was too much to think about. It would have complicated things for me. But I knew what he wanted and what he wanted was not what I wanted.

"Please tell me," he said. "Do you not love me anymore?"

I stared at him and lied, "No, I don't."

"Why not?"

"I just can't!" I cried. "Leave me alone! I have to go home now! The car is waiting on me outside and I have a plane ticket."

"Please," he said and grabbed for my hand.

I tried to fend him off but he still got a hold of it. Once he did, he muttered, "Merci."

I stared at him, remembering the first time he'd said that to me, the way it had made me feel, as if he were thanking me for something I hadn't done yet but eventually would. Now I understood it completely. I realized what he meant. It was like he knew it was over and he was telling me thanks. And the day we met? He realized it was going to be nice, great but that it might eventually end, so he was telling me thanks in advance for allowing him the opportunity. He was appreciative of our time together. And that made my heart break in two.

"I...can't," I said and felt the tears roll down my cheeks. The car was waiting, my old life was calling. I was stuck. I couldn't move one inch in either direction.

"I love you, Nina," he murmured in my ear. "Stay with me."

"I can't," I muttered. "I have to go."

I finally broke free of him and ran out the door. I ran so fast it's a wonder I didn't trip. I ran all the way to the car, to the cab which was waiting on me. I stopped and realized what I was running away from and it was from all this intense love and sex. It was too much for me and I was being a coward. But I couldn't help myself.

"Mademoiselle?" the cab driver asked in French. "Are you ready to go?"

I stared at him and then felt something shift in my heart, in my mind. What did this mean? What was I doing? Make a decision! But I couldn't. I was stuck, literally, stuck.

"Mademoiselle?" the cab driver called.

I shook my head and looked over my shoulder. When I saw him approaching, I began to cry, to hyperventilate, to thank God I'd waited long enough. I covered my face with my hands and then I felt him near me. I could smell his cologne. Then he was beside me and then I was back in his arms and then… Then everything was just fine.

"You will stay here with me," he whispered softly. "We will be together, you and I."

I closed my eyes and nodded. We would be. The panic was over and my new life was about to begin. And he was going to be right in the center of it for a long time. Maybe forever.

I pulled back and stared into his eyes, feeling the love I felt for him until it made me smile and this made him smile. I had been a fool and I was so lucky he'd brought me back to my senses.

I had to say, "Merci, François."

"Merci," he murmured in my ear and kissed my cheek. "Merci beaucoup, Nina."

www.ingramcontent.com/pod-product-compliance
Lightning Source LLC
Chambersburg PA
CBHW020630250626
47154CB00008B/2620